RAMSHACKLE
WONDERLANDS

RAMSHACKLE
WONDERLANDS

STORIES

Craig Davis

newamericanpress

Milwaukee, Wisconsin • Urbana, Illinois

new american press

www.NewAmericanPress.com

© 2012 by Craig Davis

Printed in the United States of America

ISBN 978-0-9849439-1-3

For ordering information, please contact:

Ingram Book Group
One Ingram Blvd.
La Vergne, TN 37086
(800) 937—8000
orders@ingrambook.com

I know I gave my word, but fuck it—
this one's for John Lawrence Sullivan,
who I owe a lot more…

To Sully.

CONTENTS

THESE BRICK CITIES ARE ALMOST OVER

THE NOISE RESTS between afternoon and evening. South, under I-70, neighborhoods with forgotten names are slipping out of bed, one sockfoot at a time. Here, we are smelling hot corn oil from the kitchen of the abuelita next door. It whispers across the driveway between our sibling houses. The almost oppressive air of it eases through open windows and sifts down over the little red table where my wife and I take our meals. In my mind though, I am still north of Topeka. My hair still is curly and longish. My bread—set down in warm loaves the size of fat farm cats—is airy and fine. My father and mother are home from work, working.

Here at the table, my wife pitches scraps to the dogs. Quietly, I feel this moment cast its shadow into the memories I will someday have: food and women, dogs and windows, the line of sun slanting down her forehead. Her ease mocks my past. She is asking if I'd like to go for a walk. When I look to her, for some reason I become suddenly aware of the terrestrial drift of my boyhood friends. I notice for the first time the way my love for them has stretched too thin. Too far away from this place. This terrible, immense roll of turf. A place I feel like still-frame vertigo. All around me. And I don't miss them anymore who have left. I never did. Look, the light of the sun through the window is on her face and the smell of frying has found us here. I am sorry you have missed this, my friend.

I agree to go for a walk. But I am also agreeing to my guilt… the shame of our expanse of plenty of parking. A stroll before dark, after the heat has bled off a little, skirting the bad blocks, the broken brown bottle sidewalks. Stepping down the front porch steps, the middle-western American dream circa 1900 marches out straight for blocks in a handsome, masculine line. Broken here by three stories of brick and balcony. There by statuary of La Virgen. The neighborhood is sitting on porch railings in sandals and gabacho hats, buttoning shirts from the waist to the angle of Lewis. I smell ink and brilliantine. I see the sun trip through a brown bottle tipped back into the air.

Which one of these strange neighbors tickles out this song through the open living room window? Who will send it for me from here to North Topeka, across the gulping laughter of dogs and these screaming, siren clusters of children? You? Me? All of us?

All of us a chorus are dreaming this afternoon. Me and all these people are still dreaming of parents' kitchens, of pre-pubescence, of back homes, of places with no sidewalks to guide us away, of sisters and grandfolks, of fights with my brother. My wife is dreaming of things she will never attempt to explain to me. Because the secrets we cradle are all the same. To reveal them would risk a mutual acquittal of the shames that shape us dreaming. And because—each from out our own reverie—she and I are choosing baby names. And walking with our shadows before us.

I am watching our shadows when a man the color of burnished coffee steps out from around the corner of a colonnaded apartment building. He stops short in the middle of the sidewalk. I can see her shadow nod at him politely. I swear it lightens as she smiles hello. We are turning here, down the sidewalk the man has come from. On the second story balcony, a squat woman is shaking a rug. The rug pops and the sun picks out a bead of sweat on the man's bald pate. His eyes find mine with a suddenness I recognize as the grab of the gandy. I step around him, trying to affect both deference and a posture of clear monition. I slip between him and my wife.

At the same time they both reach for my shoulder—he from the front, she from behind—and their fingers touch there. Neither pulls their hand away.

"Listen," the man says. And from the pocket of his sweatpants he extracts a small spoon, which he flips up in front of my face. I startle slightly. Frazzly cracks of epinephrine spread out over everything. The air clarifies. I feel myself swallow and force a casual smile. I can feel her hand on my shoulder like it has always been there. And I feel his hand too, resting on my shoulder with the weight of import. In the way of foreigners or fathers. I exhale.

"This," the man says, moving the spoon like a metronome. "This here a spoon. You should have one. Ought to carry it. You should carry it home...And you, miss. You gone need a spoon, too. Right? For that baby. Baby got to have a home, now. Got to have a spoon then, right?"

"Yes," she says, reaching over my shoulder and taking it. I can hear her wide, true smile, "Thank you."

"Sure you right," he says. "Oldest known instrument of human motherfucking alimentation. Go on. Carry that."

Then he turns loose my shoulder and steps back, gesturing for us to pass. He bows as we step just out of reach around him.

The woman popping her rug chuckles.

"*Qué es*?" she calls.

My wife turns her head up and holds the spoon aloft. The woman folds the rug over her arm and squints down.

"*Una cucharita*, eh?" she smirks, shaking her head.

"What's she saying?" my wife asks.

"She says 'spoon,'" I tell her.

11

The woman nods and asks my wife if she is having a boy or a girl. I translate and my wife signals with her hands. They both smile at this. The smile of the mothers and lovers of men. This I cannot translate. I do not need to.

"*La redondez le sienta bien*," says the old Mexican woman, making a belly with her hands.

"Thanks," my wife says and waves.

We turn onto the Boulevard, where the apartment stacks cede to wide, well-kept lawns and wrought iron fences. When I look back the sidewalks on either side are empty. For a second the street looks like it might run west forever. The light is gorgeous to the point of falsehood. The street runs all the way back to my childhood. Just over that crest I can feel the city dissolve and the houses spreading out until there is no neighborhood nor asphalt street. I can smell hay. Just back there—I know—is a road, flanked by ditches and sparse with homes and memory and the women or girls made them true for a time. For all time.

My wife takes my hand. The street here is wide, and the sun has her back, gambling with her hair, unfurling itself in twists of brown and blond. Some part of this sun is stashed away within her. I sometimes see it flash like fish in dark water, a swift shimmer. A pass within her pupil. Penitent, I avert my eyes from hers—deep-set, animal and calm. They effuse intelligence and kindness, as though sowing a crop whose yield is too precious to reap. I want to say thank you. I want to say wait, just a minute, while we are right here…

I say, "*Redondez*."

The bud of her stomach, beneath her bellybutton, is new and taut as a tit.

She says, "No. Definitely not."

"I didn't mean for a name. I meant 'roundness.' *Redondez*." I touch her, as one might measure a melon yet on the vine.

"What about Cucharita, though?" I stop and turn to her, laying my hand on her shoulder. Not on the top—on the side of her shoulder. "Cucharita Redondez Jones."

She peals away a laugh from somewhere holy beyond and lets the breeze float it out and away, over the bluff. High, high, high over the wide, brown river laid up to the north. Nothing is easier, nothing less weighted down.

I would, I will. I miss this place already.

MASON JAR MAKE A MAYBE

EACH HOME HAS ONE of these drives on its east side, with a little pole in the corner for the hook ups. At Oscar's mom's place there's a little garden with a white rabbit fence around it at the front end of the driveway. There are tomato plants in cages. Their vines are turning woody. Fallen tomatoes lay split and oozing into the ashy soil. A few peppers pop red and yellow and ripe from low tangles. There are a couple rows of corn. The two boys are sitting on the steps down from the door to this car-sized gravel driveway.

The steps are made of squarely stacked concrete block. Oscar's mom's boyfriend Freddy was no slouch. He set the blocks on a little four-by-four bed of sand, framed in with pressure-treated landscape timbers. There are holes drilled in the timber with a half-inch spoon bit every two feet and two-foot stakes of rebar are driven through the holes to hold the timbers in place. Freddy used a level and tapped the blocks with a mallet. Now the two boys sit on them when they aren't off and about. They sit there like city kids on a proper stoop.

Tim was there the day Freddy came over and laid them up. It was the day after Oscar's little brother Felix fell through the old wooden steps and cut open the back of his head on the wrought iron railing. Felix was one of those fragile kids. He was wheezy and he wasn't let to play outside much. He had a plump U-shaped scar on the left side of his head that stood out past his buzz-cut hair and never got as brown as his neck and ears in the summer. He mostly watched TV. Oscar and Tim could always hear afternoon soaps squelching through the screen door. If you looked in you could see the reflection from the picture strobe on the back wall like slow colored lightning.

When Felix did come outside, he had to shut the screen door without letting the latch click. Then he'd smile like he did and say crazy shit. Tim and Oscar'd fall out laughing and Felix would giggle and snort. If they got too loud, Oscar's mom'd wake up and come out on the top step which was four boards wide when it was still made of wood. She's stand barefoot on the little scratchy mat for wiping your shoes on. She'd call softly to Felix who'd go right back over to her and she'd shepherd him back inside, clucking her tongue at Oscar and shaking her hung head. If ever Tim let Felix ride on his handlebars or pretend to ride his bike around the lot while Tim held on to the back of the seat the way his dad had done when Tim was learning and Felix squealed and clapped his hands, Oscar's mom'd come out and curse him in Spanish. Shit, once she even swatted Tim on the ass when it was the second time that day she caught them. Which he told his dad about and his dad said don't go over there then if you can't follow her rules. But later when he was supposed to be asleep he heard his dad on the phone saying don't you touch my kid again, damn it, I don't give a fuck what he does.

Oscar said they had to hang out down at the creek for a little while after that. Which was fine by Tim. Then, the day after Felix fell, Oscar's mom called Tim's mom to ask could Oscar stay at their house for a few days. While she took care of some things with Felix. Tim's mom held the phone in both hands. Her voice was tight. She seemed to be breathing in too deep. She was nodding her head nonstop and just kept saying yeah sure sure anything we can do.

Oscar stayed for a while, but then his grandparents came out from California to pick him up because Tim's dad gave him chores to do like mow around the house all the way to the ditch by the road and help with burning off the west pasture and washing dishes after supper. Oscar didn't want no part of that shit and he said so. But he's a guest, Dad, Tim said. And Tim's dad nodded and said still, there's work we have to do around here and everybody has to do it, guest or not. Oscar made a sound like a horse. He looked at Tim and smiled brightly in his eyes and shrugged and shook his head like what can you do.

Now here they are on the steps at Oscar's mom's. Sitting in the whisper of dust they drag through the summer. His mom locks the screen door from inside each day after lunch. The real door is open, but the screen door is locked shut. The air conditioner drips and snores from the window that runs across the front end, where her bedroom is. The white curtains are drawn. It's hoary dusk inside there. She plays tapes in her radio. They click loudly in the middle and the tape player automatically switches them to the other side. The songs are at least newer than the ones on Tim's parents' records—most of which are jazz—but they still suck. Oscar and Tim look at one another whenever she puts a new one in the tape deck and they try not to snicker so she can hear them. The fuzzy guitars and high pitched howling die out quickly in the hot air it's so heavy. The sound barely even makes it down to the bottom of the new concrete block stoop before it turns into dust and silent hot.

Oscar's mom's place was blue-jeans blue. The lattice skirt was white. It had lacey white vinyl trim around the windows where the shutters should be. It really looked like somebody's house. She'd lock the door after lunch, when she got home from her job stocking newspaper boxes. From lunch till supper sun sink down Oscar was out there. He had a nice bicycle that his dad gave him when he went down to Wichita for Christmas. Sometimes during the school year he went down there on weekends too.

That first day Oscar stayed with them, Tim's mom drove Tim and Oscar over to Oscar's mom's to get his bike. Usually he kept it hid behind the lattice under the house against the other kids in Coachlight Arms who Tim's dad said were known thieves. Tim's mom parked in the wrong drive and when Oscar told her no mine's the blue one she let out a long sigh and put both hands on the wheel for a second. Then she put the station wagon in reverse and backed up in a wide smooth U, crunching into the little pad next to Oscar's mom's. And there was Freddy, knelt down where the steps used to be with a pile of sand and a stack of concrete blocks in the back of his pickup which was nosed in between the garden and the house so tight the passenger door couldn't have even opened. He had on a cowboy hat like a lot of Mexicans wear even though they usually aren't cowboys at all, but work for the railroad and live across the bridge in their own little neighborhood mostly where things like yards and porch paint are real particularly done.

He stood and brushed the sand from his knees and dusted his hands like the motion Joey C's dad did at little league practice when he said I am done with you fucking guys with his accent from New Jersey. Tim's mom got out of the car and shook his hand and said you must be Oscar's dad. Freddy explained and she stood a long time and looked at the pile of boards and ornamentally curved flat stock that was the old steps and handrail and she took several deep breaths and wiped the corners of both her eyes with the tips of her fingers, pulling the skin down like she was doing chinese japanese dirty knees. She said well then and opened up the back door to the wagon.

Freddy put Oscar's bike in the back of the station wagon and they took it to Tim's house and the boys rode the bikes together up and down the road where Tim lived. Tim's dad put nubby tires on Oscar's bike and they went off into the fields a couple times to follow the creek bed. In the dry scrub woods they heard animals chitter and scuttle through the brush and echoing gunshots once and the noise of the bugs at dusk was their call to head home for supper. Then when Oscar's grandma and grandpa came and got him, he left the bike because it wouldn't fit anywhere in the low sedan they drove. So Tim rode it back to him later. He rode Oscar's bike with new nubby tires all the way over to the Coachlight Arms, but no one answered the door which was shut even though lights were on inside. Tim peeled open the panel in the lattice and slid the bike underneath. Overhead he heard voices as clear as if he'd been in there on the brown and green couch. Oscar's mom said call his mom to come pick him up. There was a pause, then she said tell him he can't come in right now. Tell him Oscar's at his dad's and won't be back till next Monday.

After he built the new steps, Freddy quit coming around. Most of the rest of the summer when Tim came by on the bike his father'd put together from salvaged parts, Oscar was out there on those steps. Sometimes smoking one of his mom's skinny cigarettes. He said he didn't want to ride bikes anymore anyway, and mimicked Tim's mom saying would Oscar like to come over and play. That's what she'd said on the phone to Oscar's mom when she called. Would he like to come over and play, which is what little kids do.

Since he didn't want to tromp through the vacant lots or skid out in the gravel drives or ride over to Tim's and run the dry creek bed, Oscar mostly just wanted to sit out on the steps Freddy'd built while the afternoons saw his face and arms deepen brown. Until suppertime, when he'd stand and dust off his knees and ass. Tim quit even asking to stay for supper, because Oscar just said my mom says we're just having whatever's in the fridge tonight for dinner. Oscar'd go rap on the screen then and call Mom, Mom wake up it's time to eat. Tim would hear him calling and knocking as he rode away down the asphalt road through the Coachlight Arms. The lights'd be winking on everywhere like very boring fireworks that never faded. Tim would ride home as the dark came on and the heat lifted leaving the smell of ripe night behind it in the wind that no one else could find.

Scott Bernhard's big brother Jacob lived with his dad on the other side of the Coachlight Arms. Some of the places over there even had awnings and decks and shit. He said he'd buy Oscar cigarettes if they paid for him to get a pack too. Which obviously they did. For his part, Tim got them a mason jar of a little bit of this and a little bit of that all mixed together so his dad didn't know any of it was gone from the liquor cabinet in the dining room. They tucked that into the hollow of the concrete blocks and the hard pack of cigarettes too.

Now of an afternoon they are sitting there—for all the world like always—and between the two rows of tall parchment-colored cornstalks come two little kids on BMX bikes. The noise of the dry stems crackling is like the sound of a fire you cannot see. One of them brakes hard, plants his left foot and skids out in perfect U-shaped arc in the pea gravel. The other swings his leg over and steps off like a cowboy, letting his bike roll a few feet before the front wheel catches a wobble and the bike dives onto its side. Hey Oscar, what's up, man says the one. Oscar asks him if they want a cigarette and the kids are breathless and the one says not now, man we just had to quit because I probably got lung cancer from the last time I smoked. Oscar looks at Tim and guffaws. So Tim reaches under his perch into the hollow of a concrete block and brings out first the mason jar and then the pack of smokes which is in a sandwich bag against the rain.

The kid who probably has cancer asks what is the jar of. Oscar says poison. Poison to kill the God damn rats that keep trying to steal our cigarettes. Tim laughs and lights his. No it ain't the kid tells them. And Oscar says all right then, prove it and unscrews the lid and holds out the jar. Well what is it really says the kid and Tim says he just told you already. Doubt wells up in the kid's eyes like tears that are inside his eyeballs instead of on the outside. Bullshit says the kid. Well what the fuck do you care if you probably are dying of cancer anyways says Oscar, smiling wild.

Then the other one, the one hanging back, who is so skinny the sun's rays have hid him it seems like, he steps in front of the first kid and snatches the jar out from Oscar's hand even though it sloshes near half of it to the ground. He lifts the jar to his mouth like a chalice and takes a huge fucking gulp. The straw colored liquor runs out both sides of his mouth and then like a diving board he snaps back at the waist and vomits an arc of puke that follows him as he doubles over and splats down on the top and back of his head and on the driveway in front of him. For a kind of minute nobody says anything. Then the kid's friend starts muttering o shit o shit o shit louder and louder until he's hollering and he grabs the skinny one by the shirt at the shoulder and starts dragging him away. He turns him to go but the skinny kid looks back, wiping the corners of his mouth with the back of his hand, staring at Tim and Oscar, who is laughing like Tim has never heard a human being laugh.

When he looks over Oscar's face is all twisted up like he ate something horribly bitter and he's frighteningly, beautifully pink.

His face is the only thing in the world and it's floating, growing huge and round like the last day of the sun swallowing the dun colored world. Also he's not really laughing at all just making a noise that's almost like he's choking to death but he isn't. Tim looks away so fast he's trying not to have even seen Oscar's face like that. He tries to focus on the kids, one tugging the other up the asphalt lane of the Coachlight Arms. The skinny kid is pretty near dragging his feet on the pavement stumbling backwards but he won't quit his gaze which Tim sees now is not at them both but just at Oscar.

Then the kid's eyes flick over to him for the space of a blink. Tim blinks. When his eyes open the kid's gaze is locked on Oscar again. Tim lets out a kind of a sigh or a high moan. The skinny little bastard is suddenly smug. Scared, too. But not in the animal way. More like maybe he knows he just won something he'll always feel. Rubbing against the inside of his sternum like a knuckle. The kid is way younger than they are. Younger than Tim thought at first. He has puke in his oatmeal-colored hair. He's being dragged up the street by his t-shirt and still the little fucker won't even blink. For a second, before the kids round the bend at the end of the U-shaped lane, Tim is not even there really. All that is there of him is how scared he is to look over at Oscar and how scared he is not to. The air feels seared. Then the kids are gone from sight and still he can't bring his head or even his eyes around to look over at his friend or whatever might be there now. Jesus, what if that'd really been rat poison he says. Or piss or something. He says it straight ahead, as if the little boys are still standing there. He can feel Oscar beside him but can't look. Tim thinks all I want in the whole world right now is to get on my bike and ride it on home as fast as I can and never look back at Oscar ever again. Maybe he says it. But there is no way to leave. Right now or maybe ever it feels like. So he stays there sitting until the cigarette burns his knuckle.

Even after that he stays. He stays until Oscar stops making any sound but tucks his knees up under his chin and laces his fingers together and hangs them on top of his head. Some shimmy of light whispers between them, and now they are sitting there again. The smell of corrupt tomatoes on the ground is not moving because there is no breeze, but the dust is up anyway with nowhere to be borne to and the sling of vomit is already only a thin crust and a stain in the shape of a sloppy U on the dry gravel and it is cool inside that house but dark and there is no more lightning on the wall and who gives a fuck anyway they're sitting outside on the steps. Where it's hot and the sun is burning off time. The smell of the end of an empire is all about and school starts again soon anyway. This heat and this light that you feel and their memory in your flesh will sure as shit someday give way to winter. Winter when even the molecules of air part farther. Even so they are sitting here. As they will be, until the stoops have crumbled to clay and the planks of wood we walk on no longer take our stains.

"They forgot their bikes, man," was the only thing one of them said.

THE SHADOW KNOWS THE CORNER,
THE CORNER KNOWS THE DUST

HERE IS A SMALL CITY in the north of Spain. Around here are the towns Americans imagine, when they imagine the towns here. In September, this place is a place to be. It is green and smells old and clean in a way our nursing homes have robbed us of. He lived for a little while in a room just big enough for a bed, a water closet and a desk. He loved the room without ever knowing which way the window was facing. This is a love of place only we have learned to feel. Your lives without this love are secret pities we harbor. Outside was a blacktop soccer field where he'd watch the boys and men play in the afternoon. Bad ham and white bread and table wine, the noise of a fan with no guard.

He fell in with a few American kids around the city. On the weekends, they would take the bus to the coast just to sleep out on the beach. German men played badminton naked there during the day, but at night it was cool and up the bluff there was a town, made up of a few stores along the road. The people of the countryside, women with long gray hairs on their faces, peasants and pilgrims, smoked dark tobacco and laughed. Wash down Dramamine, sink into the rocking diesel, the asphalt road through the hills.

They walked around in the daytime, and waded nipple-deep into the cold saltwater. Some of the kids had gear for traveling. He slept in a wool blanket, curled against a big, soft woman with a Mississippi mouth. He would wake to a world of green. Everything save the sea and the sky and the sand was green, like he used to imagine Ireland. The rest was simple gray.

Not long after moving in, he was asked to leave his rooming house. His Spanish was too weak to argue, so he left for the beach with everything rolled up in the wool blanket.

He took the bus out to the little town above the beach. The waiters in the hotel café squeezed the orange juice fresh. They spoke to him in Galician, mocking his Mexican accent, and practiced their English—a scratchy quilt of brand-new cussing. He ate there every afternoon, taking away an unlabeled jug of fresh green wine every night. He was careful not to overtip.

Evergreens and palms grew side by side.

There he slept alone, between the fog and the blanket. He would wake up stiff and damp, with sand in his teeth and dew dotting the hair at the back of his neck. Rolling the wine bottles into his blanket, he walked down the shore, to a little stand that sold boiled seafood. He traded the bottles for a little plate of squid or *bacalao*. He gave his watch to a peasant in a tweed scally cap. He stripped off his clothes and waded out a way. He splashed around, and felt the prickled sea-things wash against his legs. Naked and waist deep, shivering and stiff, he shit into the Atlantic.

He was sitting on the little peninsula, leaned against the stone ruins of a house, with a bottle of wine, when the American kids returned. They offered him a little room in their flat, recently vacated by a college student who had returned home, dragging his first broken heart and his study-abroad beard back to Indianapolis, leaving six months rent behind. He agreed. To speak English again, to break bottles on pavement, the thought of these small reliefs caught him off-guard. To avoid weeping, he was forced to turn his head and exhale forcibly.

It was easy to drink port wine and imagine letters home in that close room. The newly minted man from Indiana had left behind a small wake of boyhood flotsam. Three month's rent in

CDs and a $30 set of headphones, a few sheets of notebook paper, a trashcan to spit tobacco juice in, and a few bottles in the refrigerator. A couple easy things make time seem easy, too. And they were good times, near as he could figure.

Sometimes, like all of us do, he pretended he was in prison. He sat at the foot of the bed with the wool blanket and pillow cast off onto the floor. He sat naked on the naked mattress. He did push-ups alongside the bed, his nipples tweaking cold tile. He killed the roaches and notched one, two, three, four marks and a slash in the desktop. When he drained a bottle, he padded down the hall to the kitchen, forgetting the penitentiary code of his idyll.

These things get lost easily. Sometimes he'd look around for the sort of backwash humans let flow into the places they've been. He'd peak under the bed or in the one drawer of the desk, in the closet among socks with no pairs. He found a shell casing, a seashell, and a laminated notecard with a Fahrenheit to Celsius conversion table written in blocky architects' script. He sometimes found traces of country songs collected in the corners near the ceiling. Of course he found other things, too.

There was a small window high above the radiator, near the ceiling. Usually he left it shut. It opened to the hallway that ran down the center of the flat. Across the hall another window opened, and through these open windows, he'd stage conversations with the kid across the hall, who would stand on a chair and lean out his window while he spoke in a loud voice, shirtless and tattooed.

The room was under the staircase. The tattooed kid's alarm woke him every morning. Sometimes he went back to sleep, other times he put on black socks and boxers and went down the hall to the kitchen to make breakfast with the kid, other days he didn't

25

do anything at all but lie and look at the slope of the staircase above his bed. Once he bought a cheap linen tapestry. He tacked it to the slope of the stairway above his bed and spent a lot of time looking at it. But it grew distracting. He took it down and piled it and his favorite hat out on the back veranda and burned them both with a good squirt of lighter fluid and a little too much theater. The next day, he went to the hat store and bought himself a new black scally cap. For a while after that, he quit drinking port and things seemed to subside a little.

Under the stairs he heard everyone come and go, spitting their dirty Galician, or lisping with the peninsular accent. He understood most of what they said, and knew a lot about the way they took the stair at different hours of the night or day. His hat hung on a rack next to the window, with a yellow fisherman's slicker. The landlady let gravity get the best of her garlicky weight on her way down the stairs, and when she did the raindrops shook off his hat and coat and pissed away on the radiator. Whenever she came around, he faked sleep and threw a sheet over himself and the stains on the mattress. Sometimes she came in, to explain how the washing machine worked, or to collect rent. He never saw her, but certainly she had spied him coming and going, from her perch on the third floor.

When I moved in, all this was still there. I threw out the clothes, and the poems, and kept the rest. The second night I was there, I found the tattooed kid on the veranda, crying gracefully over a small fire of clothes and notebook paper. I didn't bother him. But when he saw me, he asked if he could borrow a CD from the man's little pile, and he played it on the little gray radio in the kitchen. I poured two water glasses of thick port and tossed the hat out the window onto the flames.

Later, when the tattooed kid left, I gave him the CDs. In return, he gave me a picture of a girl, maybe seventeen, and really in her peach. In the photo, she is walking away down the middle of a street, with her head tilted to the right, and maybe turned a little to look at something up over her left shoulder. There is a canopy of what I'd guess are sweetgum trees and it is evening, and cool.

Along the street, cars are parked, yards mown, and the porches of your life line up for the roll call of an almost divine comfort. She has straight hair the color of almonds bouncing with her step. I cannot see her face, but all of us who have seen that picture know she is not smiling, but is happy. Also, let me say this…her ass is as lovely as the face of God.

I have lost this photo, somewhere between then and now, but it was tacked to the wall for all the time I lived in that room. Still, I just lived there—there in a little room, in a flat, in a house, in the north of Spain. What sort of things do we leave behind us in these rooms, where we have nested and slept? The hardest night of a life happened there, if there is everywhere you've ever been. The wind across the shore rolls the sand. The gray waves of the Atlantic sweep away our traces, the dust of our lives, the shadows we'd like to leave there. But in these rooms, we sink into the plaster and wear away the tile. On the table, the grease from your elbows has stained the wood. The smoke from your dark tobacco still colors the corners, muffling the sounds gathered there, drinking the leftover lamplight. We can never leave. There is no prettier place.

Aisle Idle, We Pine for You in Rosedale

The grocery store is a park. A place more suited to perusal than purchase. I may be alone there. I can be. Or I may be alone in feeling calmed by the endless order of only slightly different jars of mayonnaise. Among them, I understand why primitives so often refer to these stacks and rows as "goods" in their literature. How—among the wily and inexact bark of tree trunks—is a man to find something he can spread on a sandwich? Less even the hillocks rolling away in the not-so-distance. I choose the cart. Not the basket. The cart is pleasant and domestic, even if I don't really need all that much. Just to walk around among the things man has made, drifting through his atomic light, in the strange dark of a brightly lit place with no windows. I need to be free of ergonomics, and also far from women exercising outside in underwear, listening to music I cannot hear. Because I am listening always. As I wend the aisles, a lot of things are said. All around me.

Some of them talk into phones about what people they know did. Some of them swear at items in their carts that have fallen over, embarrassing themselves. There is always a handsome woman shushing a screaming child in the rumble seat. I hate that kid. Then there is no screaming, and I hate handsome. There is the sound of snot being sucked in, and the idle reading of labels.

It is cool in the frozen foods section. I wonder why the gandies don't come here and lay among the coolers, propping the doors open and their feet up. I can almost imagine them, passing back and forth a frothy can from the nearby cooler, laid up out of the tented heat of the summer, laughing heartily, but at no one and nothing in particular. Laughing as one laughs upon suddenly finding oneself happy without reason or merit. As I would like to find myself.

Instead of this, I find myself halfway into a conversation, blushing into a phone I have pulled from my pocket. I am not crazy. I cannot see the woman on the other end of all that air, but I know what she looks like. I can't picture her face, like some say they can. But I see the words with which I will describe her. She is sometimes beautiful and sometimes ugly, like most all the women I've rolled up against in the morning. She is pale and skinnier than these others. Crooked teeth. Easy and disarming her smile. When she laughs, which is often, it comes from her without warning, her eyes bulge and swim, and a noise bursts forth like vomit. She looks frightened, caught off guard. More than others, she tries to speak through laughter. She hiccups and flutters, and stutter starts some unintelligible something.

She is saying something. Now. On the phone, she is saying something.

I am thinking about other things. Really, I am not listening. It is uncomfortable, to the point of distraction, to the point of offense, to hold this thing to my cheek, and wince at her volume. I switch the phone from ear to ear, I cradle it, as I have seen people do, between my shoulder and ear. I try to look comfortable, as though I am casually shrugging. With only one shoulder. But I am not. I am not even listening. I am wondering at this disposition. She is uncomfortable, too. Her body is. She is physically unpleasant to lie upon, or make sudden contact with. Yet she is very confident, though sometimes she smells bad.

Something smells bad by the produce. Listen, goddamnit. How?

"So...?" she says.

"Sorry, what?" I ask her.

"What are you doing tonight, silly?"

"Nothing really, I don't think. You want to get together?"

"Yeah. Let's get a movie—something funny. Okay, sweetheart?"

"Yeah," I begin, "Listen I'm at the store, and I hate…"

"Did I tell you what happened yesterday?"

"No."

"Well, D'Andre called."

"Yeah?" I almost bump into an open freezer door. The glass is frosted over, except where the big side of a woman's ass props it open. I steer the cart around and she looks up and smiles. She looks back and over her shoulder. I switch the phone to the other ear.

"I think he stole my radio," she is saying.

"You told me that," I say, and it sounds jealous. This woman on the phone is not my girlfriend. Neither is the one pretending I didn't just see her reading the nutritional information on the back of a microwave dinner. I see around her upper arms there is an extra pinch of flesh. Her elbows are lost to dimples when she straightens them. I would like to pinch her, and rest my head somewhere upon her while we watch a movie.

The phone has slipped a little. I have to use both hands to steer this shopping cart straight. One of the wheels is dragging, and it wants to turn. This shopping cart wants to turn and broadside every tender fat female ass in this goddamn place.

From the phone I hear, "It's like, I just happened to mention to him that I'd left the, um, face on the radio and then when I went out there, all my CD's were gone, but his CD case was still in there, in the back seat. And, also in the back seat, too, there was his calendar, with supposedly like eight girls' names and numbers in it."

"Listen, why don't you tell me later. I'm in the store and you know how I feel about these fucking phones."

"All right, babe," she chips. "Call me later, okay?"

"Okay. Bye."

"Bye, babe."

We say bye a few more times. Tucking the phone back in my pocket, I cast about to see if anyone overheard my half of the shameful conversation. Did you heed my warning, bored shoppers?

No one lets on. The round woman appears to have found her supper. She tosses it into her cart as though it were scraps to an old, sleeping dog. She walks up the aisle and away from me. For a second, I think I see some familiar sway in the way she is walking, flanked by the glass doors, with their little plastic pennants flying out over the aisle. Like a blink, I can feel it pass more than I can see it. And it is gone. But I stand here, unnerved by I don't know what, staring as she turns at the end of the aisle and steals an almost accidental glance back. I feel less ashamed than I perhaps should. I briefly consider calling out to her, trying to explain. That I wasn't staring at her. Or that I was, but not because I wanted to touch her or see her naked. But because of something that she wouldn't believe, because it wouldn't flatter her, because it has nothing to do with her, because it was only a spark across a synapse that she was walking through, drifting through, really. Something like muslin on the clothesline, teased up at the corner, slipping into billow breeze and falling silent and still and gone from every reach of the world by my mind. Madam, you should wear looser jeans. I have groceries to get.

In truth, I only need a little sandwich meat, food for the dog, cat food. That's all I need. A basket would have been fine. Habit and comfort, maybe a good tomato. I walk the path I always walk around the store. At this hour it is nearly empty. Wives are here. Children too small for daycare. A couple of men in various stages of inebriation.

Last night, I sat at a friend's house until late. I think of this because I think of the fat woman flipping through the low-fat dinners. She had smiled, I remember.

His girlfriend had gone off to sleep. He peeked back down the hallway to their room, then turned to me and hunched down close.

"I'll tell you a story down at the shop tomorrow," he whispered. He mouthed the word 'crazy'. He paused. I breathed. Then he leaned over to me and began.

"So. I wake up last night. She wasn't there, so I get up. None of the lights were on. But I hear her talking. She's out here." He motioned expansively to the cramped kitchen behind us. "She's walking around, back and forth saying all this shit about, 'All these people—where am I going to seat all these people? A party of 23?'"

He shook his head and I nodded vigorously, as though I were a foreigner feigning comprehension.

"I mean, I don't know, man…" he said, laying both hands on his knees and pushing himself up. He grabbed two beers by their necks from out the icebox, and looked over at me on the couch. He made wide eyes at me.

"Once, in college," I said, "I woke up in the middle of the night and this girl I was with then was typing on my computer. It was a little basement place. One room, you know, and the desk was right there by the bed. I was kind of in and out of it, like you get when you're not really awake and you're not really asleep and you don't know if you're still dreaming or what. Anyway, I must have moved or said something, cause she tried to shut off the screen real quick."

"What was she typing?" he asked me.

"Some kind of shit over and over and over. Like in that movie."

"Yeah, like in…" But he couldn't remember the name of the movie either. It was late. He started to chuckle, and it took a little of the weight off. I laughed, too. Because I couldn't remember the name of the movie, and I couldn't even remember anymore how much of the story was true, anyway.

"But what did it say?" he said, sitting down again. His face lifted a little.

"I don't know, man. She turned the screen off too quick." But I knew. Later when I used the computer, while I typed, little boxes would pop up out of nowhere, like freezer doors opening into the aisles, and I would remember.

But right then, in the living room of a little shotgun cracker-box squeezed between the low slung bungalows just off State Line, sitting up late, drunk and sweaty and leaned far, far back into the overstuffed couch across from the last of my few friends, I just shrugged. We drank a little more and laughed a bit—to what, at what, I can't recall. And bullshitted about other things I don't remember, either. After a while, I stood to go.

My friend leaned back and crossed his arms. He nodded his head back over his shoulder and said, "Do you think she's big?"

"You mean fat?"

"Yeah," he said, pressing his finger to his lips, and waving the other hand down.

"No. She's big. I like that. I think a lot of people do."

"She thinks she is."

"They all do. It's not their fault."

"Yeah," he sighed and smiled. "You want one for the road?"

Here in the grocery store, the soft chine hull of her begs me back. I stop short, nauseous, suddenly washed in vertigo. The air feels adipose. Something is bearing down upon me from above, from all around. Like it's going to storm and the sky is low and fast. I feel like everything is a long way away, but closing in. I feel like I can't quite touch anything. I am dispossessed and derelict, standing stock still right there in the canned goods aisle. After a spell, as if from on high, an old woman clears her throat, to let me know she wants to get by. I move over to the side.

"Excuse me," I say.

She nods suspiciously and wheels around me.

I shake myself out and push the cart forward, avoiding the magazine aisle. Things there upset me. In the cart now there is bread, canned soup, parmesan cheese, eggs, heartworm pills, carpet deodorizer, detergent and tortillas. I backtrack for dog and cat food. And then I remember the lunch meat.

On the way to the checkout line, I pick out a good, fat tomato. When I get there, I see the big woman in line a couple lanes down. To avoid her eyes, I lift a few scented candles from the rack by the candy. One—the last one I pick up—smells like that cheap rose-oil perfume. I want to go home.

I want it to be night. I want to set that candle by the side of the last years of my life. To smell it over the wet dirt wash of late summer storms blown by, passed over, run down to swell the bilge-water creek by the rail yard. But I know where it goes, so I set the candle back and look up to meet the fat woman's gaze that

I know is upon me, laid up and heavy like the breathy weight of her body.

She is not looking at me. She is signing a check as a slim black kid stuffs the mountain of groceries—diapers, eggs, boxed dinners, chips, a four-pound package of patio steaks—into doubled-up plastic bags. She laughs at something he says that I can't hear. When she laughs, it comes out of her like vomit. But her teeth are perfectly set.

I do not know her, I remind myself. Like the drying words the wind whispers through muslin, like a glance over the shoulder of my mind, like the dreams our women imagine we've dreamt, like a skinny girl patting her lap inviting you to lay down your head…she is not there.

Still, I know where her picture hangs on the wall of the hospital, with her graduating class. She is fat and smiling and has her old haircut and her new Hollywood teeth. I know why her hair is long. I know right where that picture is, so I have to put the candles back.

When the woman leaves, I read the covers of the magazines in the checkout line. I whistle to the muzak—it is "My Cherie Amour." I haven't heard that song in so long. It is August now. How long it's been…that is like the clouds at night, the way they throw back the city lights, and you can't tell the sky is round.

"You don't know nothing about that Stevie Wonder, young man," says the checkout clerk.

I almost chuckle.

"Maybe not."

The clerk leans across the little conveyor belt and lowers his voice. He raises his eyebrows and his old brown eyes dance.

"Boy, I got me some of the best I ever had to this song. You know? Son, we was in love when they played this song, sure. Hell, and she got them old heels cocked against the roof. Had me a big old Mercury. Damn," he shakes his head, "I was in it."

"That's what it's made for."

"Believe so," the clerk grins. "Want your milk in a sack?"

The tomatoes here cost $2.50. My cart hushes itself. The left front wheel starts to turn in time with the others, squeaking meekly. I forgive you.

THE DIRT BIRDS

Mi kamocha ba'elim.
                    —Exodus, 15:11

Lament

WE WERE A FLOCK of us. Filthy. Summered. Those of us with fathers were only slightly more sheveled. Those of us without mothers were motherless little motherfuckers. Every last one. On our block Corey McCabe was as close as it got to ethnic. But to us, Corey was just another kid with a bike and his own ball glove. None of us knew he was only a generation from being uninvited to our parents' parties. Of course, there were Mexicans moving in across Roseland Boulevard and a couple of halfies here and there. One grown-up guy lived down on Elsin who was maybe part Mexican. He did tattoos for a job though, and half Mexican is like three-quarters white anyway. Plus Charlie Jones' older brother was in high school, so we were not completely ignorant of the ways of the brown people of our city. But our grandpas still said colored. Which is not too much different really than what they say now. The bougies who won't live around them. People of color, that's what they say. As though we never tanned or burnt or got dirty our wretched selves.

So maybe we were colorless little motherfuckers. Every last one. Later most of us would go to junior college or drop out of state school. By the time the first wave of divorces rolled through our ranks, we were all tattooed. Colored ourselves. We had to wear long sleeves to work, to court. We had to find our own timid verbiage for our black coworkers, for our daughters' Mexican boyfriends. By then, though, the neighborhood would be gone. As far as Midwestern white people were concerned, the entire idea of a neighborhood would be gone. And the little crackerboxes we left would be left for the non-crackers and the kind of white people—old or gay or some other lost cause—with no school-age kids. By then, Culp Elementary would have swollen with Alvarezes and Robleses and other names that people got mad if you couldn't say just right. Missionwild Middleschool and Missionwild High would see the dirty white faces and blonde lank replaced by thick braids and the diaphanous consonants of black kids trying to talk over one another.

And we'd be gone. Gone to the low-rent suburbs. The cheap, mid-century slab house kind. Nestled between the old-line, leafy, inner-ring suburbs and the new, far-flung, fake money ones. Where the bougies hire Mexicans from Missionwild to build gates in the streets. Gates to keep out the people of color—and us, too. To keep us gone. Gone to Presbyterian weddings, gone to fat, gone to custody hearings and DUI classes. Gone Republican. Long gone, motherfucker. Like the little house on the corner of Chasey and Woodson. Like the young man who moved in there after Mrs. Krakow died. Gone like girls, grace, and good work if you can get it. Gone like all the things you buy, or buy into eventually. Gone. Go on, give up, get over and get the fuck out. American gone.

Episteme

The house number was 2028 Chasey Lane. It stood on the northeast corner of Chasey and Woodson, at the crest of a steep hill. When Jude Krakow died, her sons came back to town for the weekend. They moved the furniture they'd nested in as children out onto the driveway and sold it to our parents and the gay couples come over from midtown. They put up a for rent sign, since houses in the neighborhood were too small to sell anymore. It was vacant and sporadically mown for a few months. Without notice—without even taking down the sign—on a weekday afternoon, before our parents were home from work, a man moved in. He was the first unmarried grown up to ever live on our block in a house of his own. There were, of course, some deadbeat sons grown but not gone, some single mothers whose kids were gone on weekends, some old folks who used to be married to somebody who was now dead. But just a regular dude, living in a regular house was a strange thing. So we stared. This guy was youngish, too. Not so much older than our older brothers, cousins. Not much younger than Corey McCabe's mom, whose youth itched something in our mothers and caused our fathers to cough. We watched the man empty carload after carload of stuff, stuffed into black trash bags and lidless liquor store boxes. He sweated through his shirt as we had seen our fathers do, but he never made any progress. Our fathers finished the tasks they took. Sweating and swearing, swilling Saturday, in Missionwild the motherfucking brake jobs got done, the wheels went back on, and the jack stands were returned to the garage.

This man merely made piles from piles. In the evening, another youngish dude in a shitty old pickup pulled into the drive and they hauled in a solitary load of furniture. Not even a full size pickup. They set a couch on the front porch and then climbed into the empty pickup and left. It was just before dusk by then. They left the front door and all the windows open, the living room light shown down on a mound of black trash bags. The radio was blaring all treble through the screens and the moths began to throw themselves against the meshwork. That big blue evening moved in through the calm. Cars were pulling in driveways. We went inside for supper, to tell our moms about the new guy in Mrs. Krakow's place. We were having pizza probably.

We were young and this was Missionwild, wild, wild, like that means something to you. These were the last years of rap music mattering, and yet where we lived was still the kind of place where another white person—a weird enough or new enough incarnation of white person—could seem foreign, even exotic. Even then, even as children we understood our few blocks were a bit of a throwback, tucked into a pocket of the city that had been passed by by highway bypasses and real estate realities. We knew, even then, that it was weird to walk to a grocery store for eggs. That most moms didn't let their children pack up and roam the sidewalks and undeveloped woodlots unsupervised. Sometimes Mr. Z at Z's In-N-Out would give you an extra egg, just to break on something while you walked back home up the hill on Woodson. Sometimes other kids' parents would punish you if they caught you into some shit and your parents weren't around. That seemed normal, which is now strange. What seemed strange—a stranger in Mrs. Krakow's house—is normal now, you know?

Like one time Jenny Kirchner's mother caught Corey McCabe peeking through her bathroom window. He was watching Jenny pee. Picture that, no one had the internet yet. Maybe rich people already, who knows. Anyway, Mrs. Kirchner came around the corner of the house with a rake in her hand and beat him over the head as he ran away, peeling wild laughter off of himself. Mrs. Kirchner never even told Corey's mom, who many of us had watched in windows from a spot in the woods we never took Corey to. Corey told us, though, that Jenny Kirchner wore no panties and her butt was worth it to see. Damn, she's got an ass worth getting beat with a rake for, we said that summer. The leaf kind of rake, though, the plastic kind like a fan.

That was where we lived then, in such strange shelter. And though we knew it, some of us never made our reckoning with 2028 Chasey after Mrs. Krakow left it. The house looked like it was slowly deflating. Its drawn blinds in the daytime. The way the windows were lit—one at a time—at night. The bored look of its gray asbestos siding and the exhausted shutters. We noticed the houses around it start to slump, too. Or maybe we noticed for the first time that they always had. Maybe we had never really observed our neighborhood until the young man moved in and we started to watch his comings and goings, his movements in the window. Maybe it was the first time we'd seen a window with no curtains. Maybe it was too much a part of the world that waited for us. For us and for everybody else. A kind of life that had already crept into the cities of the country, like a new accent…or more like an accent going away, our own peculiar pidgin. A life that probably existed only in nostalgia, a brief past at that. The guy who lived in Mrs. Krakow's place that summer dragged the new dross of days behind him—all our lives. Like children peeking through windows, we were only able see the meaning of it when we were running away, through our own panicked laughter.

There were those of us—Corey McCabe, the Linklaters twins Jonathon and Simon, some others—who were more worldly than the rest. The rest were less worldly—whatever that means in a world mostly forfeit. Nonetheless, the Linklaters had an older half-sister, and by then were uncles. During nice weather the cops would sometimes be called to their house late at night. Their half sister's boyfriends would stand outside her window, first pitching pebbles. Then as things went the way they would, they'd come drunk, caterwauling. Finally the warm nights would find them out there under her window, bellowing until everyone on the block woke. Our mothers would come into our rooms wearing robes, with their hair in improbable disarray, and shoo us from the windows. Then our fathers would go out on the porches and stand until the cruisers shut off their lights and went away, except one or two to take reports, again. The Linklaters' father drank whiskey at the block party but the other men merely sucked beer suds from their mustaches. And Corey Mac? He had a brother he'd never even met and he called his mother Eileen. So maybe some of us already possessed some recondite knowledge of the way things would generally go down, even then.

For the rest of us, the last year of 2028 Chasey was a story to overstate but not to understand. After all, we were young. Some of us were even children, still. Some of us were children even after the house was razed. Some raised themselves, pretty much, slowly growing up and giving up as the parking lots swallowed the corner lots and the curbs shored up the weedy runs of ditch and dirt.

Hymn

If all the house was a frame of yawning timbers, hewn from trees so long, long gone that we cannot accurately envision their span nor heighth (as they would've said when they nailed the rafters by hand—those that said *droughth* and *warsh* and *that colored boy*, those grandfathers now dead and bird in the dirt)…well, if that's all it was, then what could it have held, really? A whole life? An entire anything? Or just the flotsam a life leaves behind, sloshing in its wake like a man walking fast who has drank too much water? Our places, our abandoned places, they are houses and streets and blocks and whole cities sometimes, veined with sidewalks and streets and shortcuts through the alley easements and trails through the woodlots, hacked with machetes we snuck from under the workbench in the garage. Something still courses in the half-hollow arteries and cavities of our old places. We take some, leave some—as we are taught at the table—our dregs like sand in a sieve: the least delicate moments are left behind. There remain only the harsh words. The last generation's racial epithets. Like an honest epitaph. The too-much perfume of the women you asked to leave before the day broke. The smell of sweat that didn't dry in the sun. Dog hairs between the cushions and the dust, the dust— good God, we've been warned about the dust, enough. The dust sifting in the light at daybreak. Picture frames broke in a box and left at the curb.

A man lived in a two-story shotgun house during the last days of an epoch of us. The shutters were false—no, fake is the word—listing scarecrows of lattice. A little grey house, all day long on the corner lot. Who watched and what witnessed?

The parents of this neighborhood also eyed the house, though peripherally. They were as suspicious as we were fascinated. Suspicious because we were fascinated. Time had hopscotched our blocks. A lone white man was still a viable suspect in the minds of our people. And the blinds were always drawn downstairs. We were awed for our part. We watched the house all summer, and we came to accept it as a trope for impending manhood—a concept we understood as the graph of a line against axes of time and loss. An arc of distance between humans.

On the porch, across the street, he is enjoying a cigarette. He is out late tonight, long past our bedtime, but Corey can see the porch from his bedroom window. Is he crying? No. Singing. A kind of lullaby. We sleep. We dream things we cannot imagine: enjoying the taste of a cigarette, the sparkle of very cold beer at the gullet, sleeping drunk, parts of a girl, some human smell beneath smoke and shampoo, a cloud of her hot breath on our chests, the way we brushed her hair while she watched TV. We dream we can touch her hair, cup it, let it slide from the palm, catch the sun through the blinds. We dream it will be like coming home. It will be coming home. These are requisites with which to make requiems. These are places we go without understanding. These are burdens we will bear every day or every now and then. It's always one or the other.

Outside on his porch was an indoor sofa. The parents didn't like that. But he did keep the lawn mown. He mowed early in the morning, when the grass was still too wet with dew. Nevertheless there he was, limping behind the mower, cursing God and us when it clogged. His curses, above the buzz of a lawnmower…we woke to this.

Testament

Luke Grisnik's father's name was Ward, the mailman. He'd quit his route in Dalmatian Hill about the time old man Krakow died. The povitica the old bakas on the Hill gave him at Christmas had finally become inedible. As the women got blinder and shakier, the sugar they measured in their cupped hands took on the chalky taste of their desiccated palms. So when Ward could no longer stomach the thanks of the few Croats left on the Hill—much less distinguish the new Mexican names he had to deliver to—he put in for the route down in Missionwild, where he lived. He had the seniority, but no one else wanted the route anyway. It was almost Appalachian, all craggy hills and tucked hollers, laid up on the bluff above Quail Creek, which they all called The Crick. It was a hard, hilly walk, and he liked the exercise. Some of the bakas still called him Wiry Ward, from his time playing tight end at St. Michael's. But no one in Missionwild knew any of the old city families, so they just called him Ward, the mailman. They were outstaters mostly, come to the city for work. American immigrants, his father had called them. Most of them came a generation after the Croats and the Polish and the dagos. From the looks of it, they were only staying a generation after. On the east side of the neighborhood the hip kids and the city-gays were just starting to bleed over into the tidy blocks that bordered midtown. There, east of Roselawn, the names on the letters read like a list of endangered species. Mark Jones. Mrs. Edward Cole. James Eldon Henry. Timothy Vaughan. Sarah Grace. Then there was his own mailbox, mounted on his porch with its cursive Grisnik painted in black over a Croat tricolor. And of course the Krakow place and a couple of Mc's and Mac's. Across the boulevard, though, the new names were popping up like freckles in the summer. D'Narion Smith/Brown/Jones, Miguel Whatevero. And the second generation rednecks were fleeing back out to the cheap-o suburbs on the north side of the county, which was farmland when their parents moved to the city. You can't sweep up the ocean, his own baka used to say, when they started renting the little rowhouses on the Hill. Fuck it. He was only two and a half years from retirement, anyway. He had his eye on a place down at the lake if he could get some *crnac* to rent his place off Roseland.

Here on Chasey, the children had the run of the street. He liked that. Their stacked cackling reminded him of his own boyhood on the Hill. And the people on the route were courteous. They spoke English. They were pretty much white, even if they didn't ever tip. They were still pretty country, but they didn't try to duck collections letters or pretend that there ain't no Jack Cortland here, much less that *ya no vive aquí este mendigo.* 2028 was on his route, usually he made it around midmorning, ten at the latest. He held the few letters that still came for Jude Krakow, forwarding them himself to her son in St. Louis and delivering the new guy's frequent stream of postcards and the heaps of pre-sorteds. Mr. Our Neighbor At. He remembers the kid, and fondly. He remembers fondly a quick pull from a bottle of warm bourbon the kid was suckling on on the porch one midmorning. He remembers him on the couch out there with his feet propped on the railing.

"Yeah, he'd be out there most every day. Sometimes with that Mexican from over on Elsin. Boy, they had it good."

Lament

We didn't know him. We didn't know why, really, we watched him. Or where we would be when we realized what we had really been seeing that summer. Simply, we bore his witness. Some of us are still bearing it. Some of us were maladjusted long before, though. Most of us had moms but many were motherless little motherfuckers, regardless. You know that though. Know we were the last trod grass in a long path of childhood that has vanished. A kind of childhood that has vanished. Or been rubbed out, leaving the smear of adulthood as proof that it once pressed us and pushed us and set us out there for the world to read. Meanwhile we were not watched over. And now it feels like we were the last ragged line of uncloistered white kids in the history of all these failed cities, the great Which Ones of the American Middle West. Not that the being white part really matters. But just so you know. Like when the last native speaker of some Indian tribal language dies and you wonder, what happens to all those ghosts now that no one even understands their keening anymore?

Our own children will be, at all passes, presided. They will be kept, fenced, screened. Our parents were minded by stay-at-home mothers who never allowed a stranger to pass unapprised. Not us.

We were motherless little motherfuckers. So it's on us—who got lost in the transition from supervision to surveillance—to remind you. We went about unminded at the end, finally. Our mothers were gone and our fathers were goners. But the sidewalks were still our place. We hadn't yet been hemmed in into TV rooms and afterschool horseshit. We had our own house keys, tended our own skinned knees and a kid in a bicycle helmet was a straight pussy, plain and simple.

Sure, there were adults about, here and there. Widows who played cards in the green front rooms, or slept on the porches in wicker rocking chairs when the stillness of the air in their homes chased them out into the heat. There were sometimes fathers out of work for a week or two, always coiled and anxious and easily avoided. But they were all waiting to die or get hired. Why didn't we hide when that summer arrived? It came for us, it seems clear, in the humid air and the green pre-storm light. By July we were mired in his presence. The Chasey Lane of our childhood had become a hot bog of boredom, the kind that only a child could call curious...while from the porch of 2028, a young man's silent high lonesome begged a question. What? What the fuck are we waiting for?

We are still trying to forgive the answer: what is waiting for us.

Episteme

We were at Charlie's house. His grandmother was inside, cooking something with celery in a soup pot. The smell of it was easing out of the window and sopping deep into our souls. Later this smell—the smell of fresh soup stock—would find us, seemingly at random. It would come in a car window while lost on a side street, or await us inside a café in a small town near the cabin where we went fishing each summer. Always we were unprepared for the feeling—a little like nostalgia, but rinsed clean of self-pity—that it stirred. We were at Charlie's house and the scent from Charlie's house had spread throughout the midday as far as the midday went for all we knew.

We heard the screen door slam at 2028, felt the pulse and the push of it. It was 2:15. The old were practicing dying in the daylight. Their TVs were on loud in the houses but hushed humming all throughout the lanes and the lawns. The grass was a brittle fucking shambles. We never noticed our own sweat, if indeed we sweated. We must have been running up on August, the Midwestern month of penance. A cat yowled and came tearing out of the alley, with the Linklaters scrambling behind it waving two long sticks. The cat dashed into the yard at 2028 and the man's little hound dog brayed from the porch and lit out to intercept. The cat turned up the trunk of a hawthorn growing by the back and disappeared high into the branches. The hound looped the dry dirt at the tree's base.

The Linklaters were giving chase, still. Wild before they realized, they'd crossed the sidewalk and scrambled up the slope of the man's side yard. It was the first time any of us had set foot on his property since the Krakow's big going-out-of-life sale. The man came down off the porch and into the side yard, calling to the dog. It had a name. The dog continued braying and nervously tracing arcs around the tree trunk. In the afternoon any movement repeated can become a rhythm, a chorus soon a chant, an incantation. Arcs around the tree trunk.

Jesus, it was hot and the dog was loud.

Simon Linklater brought his stick down across the dog's back. The branch snapped. Someone gasped. Someone yelped.

The dog flattened itself against the ashy soil and shut its eyes.

"Hey," the man barked.

Jonathon dropped his stick and took his brother by the shoulder from behind. He began to back him away.

"What the fuck, kid?" The man began to stride down the yard. The Linklaters froze and stood there dumb, like odd yard art. The man closed in, then pulled up short. Corey McCabe had crossed the street and trotted into the man's peripheral vision. He moved like a pitching coach to pull a pitcher. The man turned to him.

"What's with this guy?" he asked, motioning to the Linklaters. Corey shrugged. They stood like that for a second.

"They're twins," said Corey.

"What do they only got one fucking brain between the two of them?" said the man, but you could here his voice change. He took a deep breath through his nostrils. He shook his head slowly. The dog opened its eyes and crept over to Corey, who ignored his simpering.

The man snapped to call the dog, and it was like whatever spell of fear was on the Linklaters broke. They fell to apologizing over and over each other. The man waved his hand at them, dismissing. He kept his eyes on Corey Mac. As did we. The dog licked at Corey's shoe. Corey looked down, then up at the man and shrugged.

"My popsicle dripped," he said, lifting his foot, "What the fuck?"

We came crept across the street, like kicked dogs of course. Corey stared at the man. The man returned his gaze. The smell of celery on the boil. How could the dirt be so dry and the air so wet? What the fuck?

The man chuckled.

"What, kid?"

Corey shrugged again. A strong shrug among our people is like a good handshake among others, is like making eye contact or avoiding eye contact in certain foreign lands. A shrug is a means to make measure. Of everyone who witnesses.

"Did you know Mrs. Krakow?" said Corey. The Linklaters fell silent, again, which was better. We were on the sidewalk and in the Bermuda grass holding the berm and in the shade of the Hawthorne, gathering. The dog bounced over and began to pant and sniff and jump up on us and lick. We tugged his long ears and scrunched his loose flesh. We pounded out the rhythms of big bored days repeating on his low hollow ribs. The spell was broke. It was hot still, but summer again.

"Who's Mrs. Krakow?" the man asked Corey.

"The woman who lived here," said somebody. The man looked up like he'd just noticed us, edging further and further into his yard, thumping his pup, giggling when its whiskers itched a forearm.

"Oh, her?" he shrugged. "That old hag? I killed her. You should thank me. She ate kids. Haven't you noticed somebody's been missing?"

We looked around. Somebody was always missing, we were a flock of us.

"I'm just fucking with you, kids," he laughed. We exhaled. He eyed us.

"No, I did kill her though. So I could get a lease on this sweet place." He hooked a thumb over his shoulder. "You wouldn't believe the waiting list for a Missionwild address."

Another joke, we guessed.

"Why don't you put a lease on your dog instead of your house," said TJ. We all busted up laughing. Even the man laughed.

"Jesus," said Charlie Jones, "what a retard."

The man smiled at us.

"Okay. Go on and scat, kids. I got shit to do."

Like what? Sit on your porch with the radio in the window? Walk down to Elsin and smoke a bowl with the tattooer? Yes, we know what weed smells like. People leave their windows open all summer long in Missionwild. Now that we are here, we are not going to move.

"Hey man," Corey said, "why aren't you married?"

"I'm too young."

"Why don't you have a girlfriend?"

"Why don't you?"

"Shit, I got with Jenny Kirchner," said Corey.

"Is that right?" The man bent down and picked up a horse-shoe lying in the grass.

"Yeah," said Corey, "I got some."

"Some what?"

"I hit it, I mean."

"I hit your dog," Simon butted in.

The man shot him a frown, then peeled off a deep belly laugh.

"Yeah, I got a girl, too," he said to Corey.

"Bullshit," said Simon Linklater. The man turned to Simon. He was squinting.

"No, seriously this time. She's fine, too, boy. Mmmm, mmmm. Yep. Her name is Mrs. Krakow." He paused. "I hit that, dude."

"You're a liar," joined Luke Grisnik. "Mrs. Krakow is dead."

"Nope. She's my girlfriend. We're in love."

"Prove it."

"Okay. Do you guys know how to throw horseshoes?"

The man held up the horseshoe. Charlie said he did. The man showed him the two stakes in the yard and said to look for the other horseshoes. He said to play a while, that he had to go unpack his pictures, but he would bring one that proved he and Mrs. Krakow were boyfriend and girlfriend.

"Can I come inside?" said Corey.

"No," said the man and whistled to the dog, who padded behind him into the house.

Later he came back outside. Some of us had left. Somebody said horseshoes was gay. Some others also thought it was. Somebody got hit in the foot with a horseshoe and ran home shrieking. It was widely agreed that it was even more gay to cry if you got hit in the foot with a horseshoe. We began to play a game called "try to hit my foot with a horseshoe". Gayness was measured based on how close the horseshoe got to your foot before you flinched. Gay, even in those years, was relative. Some of us were actually gay. They had to have known by then. The thought of Jenny Kirchner peeing either moved you or didn't. You would either be hit in the head with a plastic rake for love or you would take a horseshoe to the foot. Either way we were all fucked eventually, if you believe it. He called to us, stepping down the porch steps.

He was holding a framed picture and he handed it to Charlie Jones. We gathered round to see over each other's shoulders. We shoved and elbowed and grunted. Those who got a good look say that in the picture the man is standing outside a bar. There are people milling around the edges of the frame. He has short hair and his face looks sunburnt, but you can tell it's him. It's night in the picture and the light all around looks like the inside of an arcade and it's hazy. He is standing behind a girl, with his arms draped over her shoulders and his chin nuzzled against the top of her head. There are deep flows of her brown hair spilling all over his forearms and they don't have tattoos on them in the picture and there's a glass of dark beer in one hand. He's not quite smiling and the girl is leaning back into him. But where her face should be there was a cut-out picture of the little dog's head pasted over hers.

"There she is—sweet, sweet-ass Mrs. Krakow," he said.

"That's not Mrs. Krakow," Luke whinnied. "You ARE a liar."

"WHAT?" The man roared. "Are you sure, kid?"

"Yeah," Luke said, "I only went to Mass with her like EVERY Sunday forever."

"Not Mrs. Krakow, huh? Well, that's what she told me her name was. That bitch."

A scared, social little giggle ran through our circle. Corey took the picture from Charlie.

"Wow. She's got huge boobs."

The man didn't answer. He sidled around behind Corey and looked down at the picture for a while. Corey held it up.

"Nope. That's just the bra, kid." He patted Corey's shoulder.

"The what?" said TJ, clawing for the photo.

"Awright, kids. That's enough." He reached down and took the picture from Corey and shooed us. "And pick up those toys in the grass over by the sidewalk with you when you leave."

He turned away and started walking back up to his house. We headed back across Woodson. As the man was walking inside, Charlie said he saw him pitch the whole thing, frame and all, into the trash can by the driveway.

Hymn

A neighborhood of bungalows and ramshackle ranches. Split-level custody. Dent fenders. Once this was a suburb. Once this

53

was all brand-new. Now this newly-minted man, a boy banged up a bit. Skin already piled around his eyes, throw rugs in a yard sale. He was about the age of our oldest cousins, but unfamiliar. He was there that summer suddenly, like a new kind of normal, a kind which waited. A warning sign.

He was there to learn. He learned to cut the grass before the heat slipped into the day. He learned the dandelion dust. He learned to like naps on the porch. He learned our names. If you asked him, he said his name was whatever you said yours was. At first we didn't believe him. When we told our moms that he'd given us a Band-Aid for our skinned knee or pulled a splinter out of our thumb, they asked who did, now? But they were always sneaking side looks at his house. Through the blinds they watched him and our stepdads watched our moms and we left our toys in his yard for him to mow over.

Was he teaching, too? We learned also after all. We learned he would not pick up a wiffleball in the path of a lawnmower. We learned that grown-ups could not chorus as we could. Could not talk all together until the meaning came forth from the noise like a face in the static. He didn't care for our noise, our nosiness. We knew that. But he also didn't care about it. He did not heed. With his whiskey and evening air. Because if no one knew him, then he wasn't even there. We learned there were no mysteries, really. He did, too.

Just before he left, together we all learned to leave it alone. The bigger kids who played basketball in the street—the ones who won't move out of the way for traffic—they tipped their chins up at him whenever he came out onto the lawn, ushering his part-beagle onto the grass. If we asked to pet his dog, he made sure to remain in plain sight. He never let us in his house.

He sat on the porchcouch and tipped back golden cans of beer. Little runs of condensation dribbled down onto his shirt and dyed it darker. He got drunk, but not dad-drunk. He never yelled at the TV. Or threw a beercan at a car that passed too fast. He did watch them—the cars, the little ones—rolling the stop sign on Woodson at Chasey. The ghost of a ponytail in the driver's side window. He knew every red car in the city. We all know why. A ghost, a ponytail, a cast of light like a lure, a ghost, a ponytail.

It was hard for us to imagine—then—an entire day without a bike ride or a ball to toss or a new cussword to practice. It was impossible to imagine a world of letting the screen door slam in the silence after lunch. Of not speaking for a stretch of days. We could only picture him stepping inside to nap, or pitch pennies into the garbage disposal, or read the postcards the mailman handed to him all the time. It was easy to imagine these cards were from his grandma for his birthday or because his cousin was on vacation in Texas. We got those kind of postcards. But every couple days? Who could imagine that? Who could imagine this man was not our neighbor at all, but a Maccabee of many summers that rested, waited? Who could imagine a couch on every porch, on every block? A whole neighborhood where no one knows what the fuck is a divan? Who could imagine the ease with which we can now answer these questions? Imagine scribbling a question on the chalkboard and never coming back from recess. Imagine mailing yourself postcards and throwing them into the wind for anyone to read.

He sat out there late, slapping bugs with his porch light off. He ran his hand through the tangle of Spanish question marks on his head. He laughed out loud alone. We waited—though we didn't know it—for the fall. Burn the leaves.

He learned to leave. We yearned. Young. None of us knew why.

Testament

Jenny Kirchner brought her new body back from college for the summer, wider around the hips, starting to spill. She was working at the branch library again. She told her little brother Stevie that the man who moved into 2028 was there like all the time. That the man had glasses but didn't always wear them. That he checked out stacks of books from the Missionwild branch, piling them up in his arms like the harvest. Weird books. Alain de Pomme translations, a book called *Teach Yourself, Yourself*, the collected letters of Royal Elderberry, something she couldn't remember except the subtitle said "A Deep Map". Weird things. A lot of times they had to get them on interlibrary loan.

She said he went to the downtown library now, because he got kicked out of the Missionwild branch. She said that one of those bossy old black ladies that hog the internet stations came up to the front desk and said that the man and three bums were looking at porn on the 15-minute limit computer. Jenny went to the AV room and sure enough, there he was with three of the "regulars" leaning in over his shoulders. She recognized Jimmy and the fat redheaded guy that always wears the "Kansas—Linger Longer" t-shirt. She told them there was a two patron per computer rule. That they'd got some complaints, and that two of them would have to find another computer. The bums mumbled and ambled away to find an open reading table to sleep at. But the guy from 2028 turned around and asked her if she'd like to get a drink sometime. She said she didn't know why, but she said yes. She said he stood up then and pulled out a little green pint right there and took a drink and handed it to her. She pushed it back at him without touching the bottle and asked him to leave and he did. But she said he was smiling, and said, "What about that drink, though?" then winked. Actually winked.

Even then she said she kind of wanted to. She recognized him from the neighborhood. And it would piss Mom off. Especially those tattoos. She said she went to log off his computer, but there wasn't any porn on it at all. There was some website about the supposed burial place of St. James, in some country called Galicia, and she thought, damn, if I'd have known he was Catholic I would have invited him to dinner and told my mom I was going to start going to church with him.

Even Stevie smiled at this, that simple motherfucker.

Lament

Not even our parents will die here. This block, where people died in the front bedrooms for an American forever. We didn't leave much for the people who moved in here after we didn't come home from dropping out of college. We let our parents' houses peel and warp and bow. Though, what we did wasn't really leaving, so much as we just didn't go back. We were losing our first good women, our first minds, the last of our real friends. And we never had much history, really. We were just garden variety crackers. The kind you don't even get to explain what your name means or which of your great-great grandparents is from what county in Ireland where you've never been. So fuck it. We threw in the towel. Bought into the unbrave but almost brand-new world. Where there are children everywhere that no one ever sees. And when they couldn't climb the front porch steps anymore, we found places for our parents out here, close. But if ever we need some strange industrial part for something, if we want some Mexican food in a place with grime in the grout, we'll drive through Missionwild sometimes if it's sunny. We'll point out the window to the old house, to Culp Elementary closed, to the old alley easement between the lots. The houses will be painted those colors people of color love so much, and the boys on the sidewalk will meanmug us. Fuck them, though. We still ain't scarish. Don't let the County tags on our cars fool you, punk. Our kids talk your slang and we know they're soft as hell.

Mid-block there'll be a couple new places, tasteless…just like ours, but looking strangely failed already. Out of place. Garages will have been added. The doors will be off track. The corner lots will all be places to park. New exterior staircases will sprout. New doors to the second floor. Letters and ½'s will have been added to addresses. Young white men who aren't from here will be in every fifth or sixth house—wearing shorts and no shoes—sitting out on porch couches, playing guitars and smoking weed in the daylight, waiting. Waiting for their women to pull them back to where they came from. Some of them will wait too long and when the gentry start bleeding in even this far west—all the way to Roseland, in fact—with their paving stones and perennials, they will find these leftover men still here on the sagging balconies, sunburnt and bearded, dragging back and forth to dishwashing jobs at the cafés on 44th and they'll price them out and send them slouching into the next slum of color they can afford to ignore.

We had no idea we'd be among any of them, but we were. They dragged us, we dregs, leaving scraps from our pants caught on brambles, leaving broken bicycles and bottleglass shards in bare feet. We left evidence. But we never left. Here. Right here. On the left. Look, Corey. Where that little red car's parked. That's where Daddy's old house used to be. And that's where my friend

Corey used to live. Did you know Daddy had a friend named Corey, too? I think that was his name. Maybe, Kasey or K.C. or T.J. God, I can't remember shit anymore...fuck it, who wants some tacos?

If there are any of our old lingering longer, they will be inside hiding from the weather. The new nameless grown-sups of the neighborhood do not come out until late at night and anymore we won't go down there after dark with our families in the car.

Episteme

When we realized the man who lived at 2028 was gone, when we'd watched the house for three straight days, and Charlie Jones confirmed that no one had stirred within for two nights, someone tried the front door. It swung wide, and we walked into the dimness, lemmings. Who turned that knob? Turned us into what we became? What freckled hand offered that apple? What the fuck, we thought. Inside we felt different. Different fear found our boys' hearts as we braved that mellow dark, dank mildew. We were exhilarated. We'd sought this fear for so long—in wooded lost lots and crawlspaces—fear that permeated things instead of slipping their surfaces, fear that you could feel cast its shadow forward into your life. We knew when we walked in we had found it, and without speaking we were trying to measure its mark.

Corey McCabe went through the door first, we're certain. He said he'd been inside before—when Mrs. Krakow lived in the house—and knew his way around. He said she used to run her air conditioner all afternoon and she asked him would he like some Kool-Aid and he said yes, even though his mother once said Kool-Aid was for niggers. This we remember clear: she said it loudly, for all of us to hear. We'd always thought that was strictly

59

a father-type word, like cocksucker, or broke. Eileen McCabe on her porch in cut-off jeans and a bikini top, with her coffee-colored hair and her low, slitty eyelids, smiling and beautiful when we gasped at this. So we flocked behind Corey, fanning out. For a while, at least. The back of his head was pink where the sun-burned scalp showed through his mouse-brown buzz cut. There were slashes of dirt in the creases of his neck. He walked slowly at first, light pooling around him in the dim, making a halo as it bled from the corners of the room. The smell was not something we could identify then. It was not drought-toasted grass and it wasn't the thinning, tinny air of blistering winter. It wasn't the smell of finished basements or plastic packaging. It wasn't class-rooms or homes where your mom smoked inside or the gasoline smell of a closed garage or the all-over smell of dog shit colluding with the sweat-logged air. The home smelled like a world we'd never entered. Like a word we'd never utter.

But there was Corey Mac, waltzing through the waft. He be-gan to pick things up. Random objects, beyond identity, he passed them over his shoulder to the crowd of reaching hands clutching from the shadows. Jesus—those were our hands. Then Corey began tossing shit, just flipping things off to the side like Frisbees. We all began to throw, hurl, break things. Thumps and thuds and the perfect music of glass shattering. Still no one spoke. People grunted, got hit, cut their hands, and not a word passed between us.

We moved out then from behind Corey and swarmed, an orgy of small tearing hands, the upholstery rent and the stuffing gnashed, tables were upended wholesale. Someone climbed the bookshelves and leaped from the top with shriek and the muffled voices burst out of us, as they always will when young boys or men congregate in too small a space to hold their hearts and we began—all of us—to scream and yelp and open our throats to the noises that don't have names, noises no animal would make because they are sounds without subjects, the noise you imagine the universe makes as it pushes out against the…what? The nothing. That's what it sounded like inside 2028, nothing. Maybe it was actual silence we were hearing and had never known it before. Bared teeth and tortured contortions and mouths stretching spit from their gapes, our eyes unblinking, shrunken blue irises. We were not yet old enough to drive and some of us couldn't even ride bikes yet and the music on the radios of this city was rap when it was wonderful, and believe it: we were born for this.

And yes, it subsided. The blinds were torn from the windows and it was light inside. We hadn't left the front room. But Corey had. The light cast a sloping rectangle through the doorway to the TV room and caught Corey's legs hanging off the couch. We pushed through the door and our eyes readjusted and there was Corey, sitting, staring. Without looking he reached a remote from off of the armrest and thumbed the power button. We began picking up the things of this room, too—turning them, weighing them in our hands. We were passing them on. Corey's thumb tapped out a code on the remote, but the TV never came on. Corey continued in a daze. As if he were watching Minor Megaflock on a Saturday morning in his PJs. He reached out with his left hand and laid it on a sleeping dog curled on the cushion next to him.

There in the dark we set to. We made a pile on the carpet of all the man's little possessions. We began calling dibs, divvying, shoving things into our pockets. No one said anything to Corey. We moved in loping circles around him, as we did our fathers when they sat in front of football games. Who noticed the dog was dead? Did we know from the time we came in the door that

61

the dog was guarding another threshold beyond? Did anyone confuse its presence for the presence of mere slumber? Maybe the younger ones. Maybe there weren't any younger ones at all. Maybe Corey McCabe was never there in the first place. It's hard to say. Who was that boy with the crust of dirt and sweat and peeling pink flesh on the crests of his ears? Was the TV on after all, weren't TVs always on? Were flashbulbs bursting inside the framed snapshots of the brunette on the wall? No? What slow lightning, then, cast stark, sudden shadows on the boy sitting stoic on that sofa?

Huh?

Light was cutting in through the blinds, here. Shelves of it fell across the wall opposite the windows. No one went up the stairs, though. No, never. The linoleum in the kitchen had a single set of bootprints in the dust leading in that never came out. The linoleum in the kitchen had a handsome pattern of glyphs repeated on its grid. Patterns repeated in that kind of light trace runes, trace ruin, trace patterns repeated in that kind of light. The light was coming from somewhere and Corey McCabe was occasionally chuckling, but no one noticed. There was a lawnmower buzzing up the block and the noise of a road crew banging the big bucket of a backhoe against the blacktop. The silence—if that's what it was—had quit us again, forever this time.

Jonathon Linklater, whose deep awkwardness was evident even then, poked the dog's eyeball with his finger. The entire eye gave way and he began to twist his digit further and further into the dog's eye socket. It bottomed out at the knuckle and he lifted his face to the rest of us with a look of hope and wonder we'd never seen in the face of a person old enough to speak.

"Holy shit," he said like a grandpa who farts in church without knowing it. Corey McCabe turned his head, then, and lowered his eyes down to Jonathon's hand, knuckle deep in the dead dog's eye. He lifted his hand from where it rested on the dog's shoulders and gripped Jonathon's wrist. As he pulled Jonathon's arm up, the finger came sliding out of the socket with exactly the noise you'd imagine, coated in what looked like merely mud in that light. Like that they paused. Corey with Jonathon's hand aloft—eyes locked—frozen like ballet dancers waiting for the music to cue.

Somebody spooked then. It spread through us like contagion. Someone, as though tapped on the shoulder, turned and dropped into a dead sprint for the front door. The noise of the screen slamming broke the shroud of reverent quiet that had swallowed us. Before we could blink we were again shrieking, scrambling for the door, pawing at one another to weasel through the narrowing jamb out into the sunshine and the slavish humid press of the summer we'd left only minutes ago. We regrouped across the street, on Corey's corner, by the fire hydrant his father had painted in the colors of the Irish flag to cover up the Mexican gang graffiti that the city'd left there for a year and a half. In case it's not clear, Corey McCabe was not among us. Simon Linklater swore up and down that he'd never even seen Corey go in, that he was not there. Then he put his arm around Jonathon's shoulder and walked him up the street to their house without a look back at us, talking low into his brother's ear. They were twins, it was hard to tell them apart from the back or in low light.

No one spoke. For a while we stared at the house across the street. Then by ones we peeled off and headed up or down the hill to our own yards for the rest of the day and some days after. We carried away from there pocketsful of artifacts, though. In total, we kyped seventy-six postcards the man had addressed to himself, seven of which were postmarked. Plus a hen-scratch sketch of what appears to be the dog, sleeping as we found it. In a similar hand, a list of names, some of them ours. A magnet in the shape of the state of Ohio. An unlabeled VCR tape. And of course, other things. Lungsful of air from inside the house—dust from another idyll—doghairs on our clothes. And things that cannot be weighed at all but can only be charted. Things we lifted and stole that are really just deviations in trajectory. We stole the waves that would wash us. We took things we could not carry, some of us. And we took things that were always ours, others. A duffle of masks and maybes.

What we took were warning signs we could not read.

Hymn

It began to cool at night. Cool enough to imagine. So, we imagined her as we imagined he had. Out front of a home, at whatever age we were then. She had big eyes and bright forehead. She walked bouncing without grace. We imagined watching him come out to meet her on the porch. We could see her reflection in his pupils. We imagined her as a child and as a mother, but we could not imagine her in between. We could not image what happened behind her eyes, when they finally took on their hardness, their distance, their true beauty. We were only children, still. We had never known a woman, only girls and moms. We couldn't hear the things she said to him. And anyway, they don't bear repeating. Soon enough, sons, we needn't imagine. Just a few more falls.

In the evenings, children grew. Their shins ached against the deposit of calcium, the invisible construction of bridges between cells untold. The wives spoke low into phones when the kids walked through the rooms. The weather found forgiveness in its heart after all. The mail came, tight and perfect with pre-printed addresses. The dandelions and the clover choked the grass without effort or spite. Every night someone was passed over. The nurses in the ER snickered about sick patients' poor taste in shoes. Calm things came idling through our lives while small radios thinned basslines. Baseball was dead. In the Midwest we remained modest and outmoded mostly—we shrugged it off. Meanwhile, on somebody else's block, a young man leaned back against a brick balustrade, trying to catch a spark to the sweaty Bic, trying to worry about water pressure or back rent or anything else at all. Remaining reminded, depite best efforts, of whatever it was that was left. When he left, he left us all, throwing rocks against her window in our mind.

Testament

The good life was going on at 2028, they said. A med-tech who worked at the hospital remembers stopping by one day, to ask about renting the house. She recalls the man who came to the door as not knowing shit about shit. He didn't even know there was a motherfucking *FOR RENT* sign in the yard. She recalls him as being polite but not paying her no nevermind, at first. She means his solitude was not a bubble you could pop. She means when she knocked on the screen door she could see him inside dancing drunk and that he didn't stop when he saw her standing. That he seemed like he had an extra sky around him of calm, low-grade tragedy, and that he was living with it and that it made her feel all discomfited even if she can't say why. Through the screen, she remembers, the most beautiful music was playing. It was something old and slow and sad. Muffled by the weight of the afternoon air, the voice on the stereo came through like a hug from a big man.

"I told him, go ahead. Go on and keep dancing. I told him I didn't mean to fuck up his groove. Then you know, I aksed him could I step inside. Girl, do you know he even fixed me a drink. I aksed did he have some ice or some red pop or something to mix this with. He didn't, but I give him my number, anyway. I wrote it on this postcard he had had. One that had a note already on it. I wrote it down anyway. Even wrote 'about rent' next to my phone number—case he had a woman and she found it, you know."

She said he was a all right dancer, too. Never did call her though. You know how them white boys are. All brave and shit when they drunk but just can't seal the deal. She was as surprised as shit when Ken Krakow called her that September to see if she still was interested in renting that place on Chasey. But by then she had already found a place to stay just the other side of Rose-land and its some more black folk over here, anyway. Nobody but Mexicans want to live around all them low-wage white folks. They dirty as shit.

Lament

2028 Chasey was raised, two straight stories of balloon-framed studs, by union carpenters in 1926. We were raised in more ambiguous times. Birthdays were fixed but the years were fluid. Our records are only old postcards, sketches of dogs, hieroglyphs in the linoleum. Fire hydrants painted in the banners of Republics we'd never see, not even on maps. Plastic figurines mangled by lawnmowers. When you made the new world without porches, you wrote the days without mothers, you simple motherfuckers. We went to public school and we die in car wrecks. We talk like this because our fathers didn't talk to us too much. Watching the wall of 2028 Chasey as if it were real.

Listen, Luke Grisnik was—and is—a liar. To this day, no one knows TJ Nash's first name. A kid named Corey McCabe died on an ER bed not five blocks from his own house while a show about ER doctors blared from the television in his empty house. But no one knows what he died from or when it happened. The McCabe's always left the TV turned on. Timmy Vaughan married young and moved to Southtown, sent his kids to public school where they got jumped almost every beatdown day. Charlie Jones' kind of had a black folks' name and maybe that's why he went wigger in high school. The Linklaters were twins, which is probably the strangest thing a person can be. We grew up.

The next spring the hospital bought 2028 Chasey for the corner lot. It had sat vacant for the whole school year. Missionwild Mexican sets had tagged the whole west wall with indeciphers. Workmen stripped the wiring and the house was razed in the course of a school week. The graders and pavers and scab finishers rolled in like ants and left a parking lot in their wake and a sign that said *Reserved.* A warning sign. The nursing students parked there: twenty-something girls who were—to all the world—women. Their smoke breaks were already at the corners of their mouths, tugging like toddlers on pantlegs. Their future was shorter haircuts and rings so tacky that we'd laugh...if we weren't the ones in debt behind them. Of course there would be little red cars parked there. There'd be girls with their hair pulled up high on the back of their heads. Their laughter already throaty and tinged with meanness, their eyes flinty when they sparked. Yes, there'd be girls as summer slipped. There would be another fall, for some of us—for some of us, still.

Apocrypha

It wasn't long after the man left and we'd tried his door that Char-lie Jones' Dad let him start driving. Charlie, as his older brother had, disappeared from our lives then. He was transferring to a Catholic school for 9th grade, and his parents enrolled him in a late-summer, two-week class to try to catch him up. They let him take the hatchback to school and back. In the morning, we'd see him back out of the driveway, weaving like Mark's dad when he came home from the Missionwilder long after supper. Then Char-lie'd disappear over the hill dragging tinny, West Coast, gangsta rap bullshit behind him like just-married cans. After lunch, while his parents were gone, he'd pull back into the driveway with a carload of Mexicans and white boys, all in white polos and khaki pants. They'd go into his house with backpacks and come out in the mid-afternoon dressed like black kids, practicing their slang and waving the back of their hands about while they shouted from their necks. Then they'd pile into the two-door car and weave up the street without so much as a thrust-up chin to us.

So we were a bit taken aback when Charlie backed down his driveway one late afternoon and rolled down the window, press-ing it down from the top with his right hand and jerking the han-dle with his left. They were passing a joint around and Charlie took it up between his thumb and index finger and waved us over with his three free ones.

"Hey little man," he said, lifting his chin to Corey McCabe, "Let me get at you, dog."

Corey stepped to the front.

"Look here, son," Charlie said. "I saw your man that other day. Dude from that house, man."

Corey squinted.

"Word, son," Charlie sucked at the joint and passed it to the smiling Mexican next to him.

"Hey, dog," said the Mexican, "You nigger-lipped that shit, dog. For real."

"Shut the fuck up, Tony," Charlie said. "Damn, dog, I'm trying to school this little motherfucker right here, dog."

Every time some one said the word *dog*, Jonathon Linklater flinched.

"Anyways," Charlie singsonged, turning to Corey again, "your man stay up on Michigan street now. You know, in them big brick apartment houses off of 43rd."

Charlie snorted. The boys in the back seat leaned forward.

"Your man say tell you," Charlie coughed out a quick, violent laugh, "Your man say to tell you, you can have that bitch, man."

Laughter erupted from the car and Charlie shook his head and held his fist to his mouth. Then they pulled away. Corey McCabe looked up the street after them.

"What bitch?" asked Jonathon. "The dog? That kind of bitch?"

"No, man," said Corey.

Jonathon's eyebrows drooped and his shoulders sank.

"Oh," he said. "Damn...dog."

Corey asked who had the picture.

"What picture," we said.

"From the wall," he said. "The one above the TV. From inside the house."

No one had it.

"Bullshit," Corey said. "Who took the picture from the wall above the TV?"

Nobody.

"If you want it so bad," we said, "let's just go in there and get it."

"Yeah," said Jonathon eagerly, "I want that dog's collar, anyway."

"What fucking dog, man?" asked Corey, and turned to Jonathon. "What the fuck are you talking about?"

"You know. The little one. On the couch," said Jonathon.

Corey shook his head like a bug had lit on him.

"It ain't in there anymore," he said.

"Well, we could still go," said TJ, "We could get that girl's picture."

"It ain't there either."

"How do you know?" we asked him.

Corey didn't answer. He sat down on the slope of his front yard and stared across the street at the blank gray side of the house. After a while someone brought out a glove and a baseball and we tossed pop-ups to each other in the street. We drifted down the hill away from Corey and the house until a little red car turned onto Woodson where we were bouncing each other grounders. The car honked. We parted. As it passed a woman in big sunglasses twinkled her fingers at us and flashed a wide, white smile. The car climbed the hill and slowed in front of Corey McCabe, who was still sitting on the crunchy fescue hillside, looking up at the empty side wall of 2028. We saw her head turn toward him though the back window. Her thick ponytail swung after and splashed around inside. Light from the sunroof caught in the brothy warp of it. She rolled down the passenger side window and Corey stood, dusting off the seat of his pants and cocking his thumbs in his back pockets. He let out a sigh that breathed down the hill toward us and leaned back on his left foot.

Luke Grisnik, the mailman's kid, came over the hill on his bike at a crawl and began to pick up speed, letting the bike pedals idle and the wheels spin free after he crested the hill. We were planted on the sidewalk on the east side of Woodson, by the old overgrown alley easement in between Chasey and Elsin Street at the bottom of the hill. Corey was standing across Woodson on the west side of the street. The sun had folded his shadow up onto the passenger door of the little red car. Luke flew by, coming down the hill between us and the lady's car, passing in front of that yawning pause. Something threw a glint of sun in our eyes, like a camera flash. Or a spoon lure.

Here it's difficult to say what happened. Probably nothing. What we told our parents—and later the police—were versions so wildly different that some of us were threatened, some of us punished, and some of us dismissed summarily. What we know for sure is that Luke Grisnik didn't see shit, no matter what he says. He was riding northbound down the hill, rounding the hard right turn onto Elsin where Woodson ends in front of the apartment complex. Which means he was looking the other way. Luke Grisnik is a fucking lying Dalmatian Hill polack. A full of shit St. Michael's Catholic school kid.

Jonathon Linklater says the lady pulled away slowly, still looking at Corey and couldn't have seen the dog. Simon shushed him. Mike Morris says she opened the passenger door and the dog jumped out as Corey got in and that the dog got its tail wrapped around the axle or something as the car pulled away with Cory Mac in it and that he saw the dog get rolled all the way around the tire, head lolling out between the wheel well and the rubber. Mike Morris had the first filthy wisps of a mustache and he still watched cartoons. TJ said the car never stopped. Timmy Vaughan told the cops that Corey McCabe did see the dog, but that it wasn't the lady's dog and he don't know where it came from. Timmy said Corey saw the dog but then looked up at the gray house like he was asking permission for something—his words. He said he looked to see what Corey was looking at and that he would swear on his mother that the blinds were parted in the second-floor window. He later went so far as to claim that Corey never got in the red car at all, but that he had kind of snapped to at the last second and tried to dive for the dog before it ran under the car as the lady started to pull away and that the back of her car bounced up and down—just like those cars the Mexicans have do—as it rolled over Corey and the dog, both. Tim Vaughan looked us in the eye and the cops too and told us that then the lady stopped the car in the middle of the fucking street and got out with the car still running and the door thrown open and began screaming and scooped Corey up in her arms like a big bag of dog food and laid him in the passenger seat and took off straight up Woodson toward the hospital as fast as she could and that the dog just lay there in the street with a flat part in its middle and that that's what made him start puking.

Applied Exhaust Theory

THE DEEPEST PART of night passed. Monica came up the stairs a little drunker than she wanted. Her shirt front smelled like rubbed-on man, her breath fruit rot. A man had dropped her off in front of the building. Mark, maybe. She should have let him walk her up to the apartment, but that kind of theater seemed unnecessary. She wanted to lie down on her bed with the smell of him all about her, though. Or the smell of men, some man. She wanted to dream a little about men, and drift off. She wished she were soberer, but she was glad she could be alone for a bit before sleep. This man would call in the morning—probably Mark, she reminded herself—and he would tell her his name then. Usually it was the first thing they said when they talked.

She was glad now not to have to listen to a man talk, but to still get to smell one on herself. I should brush my teeth, she thought.

The first part of morning at the end of night feels like a kind of big noise is happening, but without any sound. The weight of the air changes. Full morning would be upon her in a few hollowed out minutes. She tried to wish herself sober so she could feel the exhaustion creep into her—a slow, sex-type feeling that started in the arches of her feet and behind her knees, the valley of the spine... all her hollow places. The washed-out ache of the forgotten muscles she'd used in bed. Strange small muscles in her lower back and the ones where her hips met her abdomen.

She sighed in the fluorescent light of the hallway and dug for keys in her purse. Without knowing why, she startled. Spun around. Behind her the hall looked flattened and shallow. The light seemed to have soaked into the space where shadows should be. Textured walls and the narrow, brown boxes of doorways framed a split flight of stairs: half leading down, half leading up. The stairwell sheltered the only suggestion of depth in the scene. Her shoulders relaxed. She felt a sheer wisp of disappointment slip from her body. The hallway was as empty as when she'd passed. She swore, though, she had seen or felt something there behind her. Maybe it was a ballast flickering or a door opening somewhere in the building that she couldn't hear. Some change in the weight of the air. Maybe it was time, breathing.

That used to happen around Jacob. The pressure in the room would change when he walked in. Even outside, clouds and light and the churning white noise of the world would pulse a little when he came into it.

She exhaled. She stopped as she got the key in the lock, paused before she turned the knob, looking down. Her hair fell beside her face. She was blindered, off-balance, drunk, vulnerable. Her guard was down. Now would be the time to slip up behind her and take her by the shoulder and turn her. She would gasp, but would not cry out. He would stare at her without speaking, his eyes floaty in their fleshy lids, whiskey on his breath. Jacob. She'd practiced how she would look at him. No feigned lack of recognition. No surprise. No artifice. She'd practiced. Just a very neutral size-up, a nod—not quite curt, not quite not—to show she'd been expecting him to come to her in the night, some night. Whatever weird, mildly sloppy shirt he'd have on. His comfortable belly and his broad shoulders and his thick-tined ribcage. She knew just how much wistfulness to allow in her gaze. She was ready for his hand. She waited. But again it didn't come and she turned the knob. A little too drunk, maybe. And too flushed still with the rut, and the scent of her new choices tussled in the velvet of her brunette hair and the haphazard buttoning of her blouse and the hand-sized welt on her butt cheek.

She looked down. Maybe there'd be a letter on the floor. Slid under her door, spotlighted on the dark stage of the living room floor. But the light caught nothing but the nap of the cheap carpet. She dropped her purse on the little table and hooked the door chain behind her. In the dark she felt her way along the hallway to the bedroom. Her roommate was snoring behind the door as she passed. She felt a quick pulse in her throat. Vomit or a sob. She sometimes couldn't tell. It passed and she got to her bed. She pried off her mules and unbuttoned her blouse again. She caught herself wishing Mike or Mark or whatever were here to take off her clothes for her, then leave so she could sleep.

She lay down, awash with the internal slipperiness of hard liquor and sugary mixers. A little sore now, already. Her roommate's snoring was escalating. Occasionally it caught, paused, then resumed. She snores like a man, Monica thought, nestling into her pillow.

Sleep began to gather in the room like the nightmares of children, but disappeared every time she drew near it. Something in the folds of light was hiding. His noise and his skinfeel on her fingertips, his boyish, diffuse discomfort and his occasional hardheartedness. Somehow the memory of these things had followed her, stalked her, found her out, as though she were the one hiding...hiding here, in her own apartment, in the room in which she slept. Jacob lay in wait—or the memory of him did—in the valleys in her body where sleep slips in, in the folds of light in her room. Now, when she was drunk and exhausted, when she'd waited for him to find her so many other times...now, he made his presence known, and for once she could not sleep.

There was no one to call at this hour. Usually she had wrapped into the warmth and breathy funk of sleep by now, and woke in the broad, open light at midmorning, to pad about in the comfortable business of her life. Usually the sun was on her side and the nighttime was full of other distractions: the rest, the roosterism of boys, the restoratives that women learn to keep in reserve—mothers and blood and comfort. Secrets among the many more. Now she was awake without the world to happen all around her like a blanket for the waking mind. She was bored. She waited.

The popcorn ceiling cradled her thoughts and half-dreams and slowly she could feel sleep coming in like the dew between the hills and gathering the room into its flat blue-gray. If she paid no attention to it, she could feel it creeping closer, as though it were an animal slinking toward her when her gaze was averted. It would startle and freeze and retreat if she were to look at it directly. Finally it displaced her ambling thoughts, the leftover smells teasing her nostrils, and the discomfort of desire on the skin of her mind.

A loud, barking voice outside her window pulled her up from some start of dream. She sat upright and leaned to peek out the window by her bed at the asphalt parking lot and the long, low row of carports. She couldn't see anyone at first. But she was looking for Jacob. He would be standing down there in the gravel and the scrawny spirea at the bottom of the stucco-paneled wall, hands in his pockets, elbows locked. She slid open the window and leaned her head out to look down. The sidewalk was as empty as a hallway. She wondered if maybe Mark or whatever his name was had come back to beg for one of those miserable, second-pass, morning-time dry fucks. The first date boys can't give up on those.

When she heard the woman's voice it was thick and reigned in for quiet. Even so, it was dense with intensity and Monica scanned the lot until she found the source of all that bunched-up, muffled rage. There were two bodies leaning over the roof of a little car not far from her window. She couldn't understand why she'd missed them. It was not Jacob. They were two just-out-of-high-school kids—the boy skinny with a big pile of curly light hair and the girl in a wife-beater with big old fake boobs mashed onto the top of the car and her hair was piled up and trashy.

Without thinking, because they were young, and because the boy didn't look like him and the girl didn't look like the kind of girl he'd like and because the car was little and newish and probably foreign, she leaned out the window to hear better. Jacob liked short girls, a little round, girls with the kind of asses black guys drool over. He hated fake boobs. He'd sometimes check out trashy girls, but she only ever saw him look—really look—at the cuter ones, not the whore-looking hos like that one down there. But maybe when she saw him next he'd be with a slutty girl, though. She kind of liked that idea.

Jacob and her had been out to eat once in a phony little bistro-type place in a strip mall in his home town. The kind of place with one wall yellow and one red one and polished concrete floors and arty sticks and twigs in square vases on the tables. Jacob's eyes kept drifting over her left shoulder. It was early for dinner, they were going to a movie or something. The light was coming in from the big window in the front and now it nested in the peachy hairs above the shave line on his cheek. It was bright and his skin was drinking in the color of the fall, the tone of that part of the earth, with its easy dun color and its russet and a color that gold wishes it was. A color that the uninterrupted sky ushers into the world there in late September. A light the people of that place never leave when they leave there. A light that makes them ashamed to have ducked such beauty.

Monica had had on a sweater and she knew her boobs looked good that night because she was about a month and a half pregnant, just starting to plump and push against her bra and it was sheer and she was probably even nipping out a little...it was cool in the evening already, and the restaurant had front windows that opened like garage doors. So she had wondered what he was looking at, but she didn't say anything or turn around, because the last time Monica did that, it was a painting he was staring at, and he made her feel like a jealous bitch for asking. Instead, she excused herself and went to the bathroom down a long hallway at the back of the dining room and when she came back into the room he was looking and it was pretty easy to see at what. The girl he kept sneaking looks at was just barely officially fat, which Monica had actually found pretty comforting, given her situation. The girl had a tall, slightly shiny forehead curtained by very thick hair the color of iced tea in the sunlight. Monica had to admit her wide eyes were absolutely gorgeous, almost Russian in that almost-Asian way. She was dressed like a girl who just put on ten pounds and hasn't quite had the courage to buy herself new, bigger clothes. As Monica watched, the girl pushed out a loud stage laugh with her head thrown back and her throat on display and laid her hand on a man's shoulder. When the girl settled down she gave the guy what they both probably thought was a real fuck-me look, but first she eye-checked Jacob to make sure he was still trying not to watch. Monica snuck up behind him and laid her chin on his shoulder and stared right at the little slut until she looked back over at Jacob again and saw Monica's face next to his and then, while she held the girl's surprised gaze, Monica mouthed the word *bitch* in as brazen a way as she could muster. The woman rolled her eyes and turned back to her gayish man.

Jacob had leaned his head on the side of Monica's face and he must of known she immediately lost her hot rush of rage.

"High school girlfriend," he said. Monica patted his back like a teacher and sat down. Then she turned her whole body in her seat, resting her arm on the low back of the black wooden chair and gave his high school sweetheart an up-and-down so catty she was a little embarrassed and a little proud. The woman looked away again quickly and Monica saw her in profile. Definitely pretty. In her way, she looked very...open. Maybe a little desperate for attention, but those small-town bitches never learn there's a world that cock can't give to you. She turned back to Jacob.

"Cute," she said. "What's her name?"

Jacob raised his eyes to meet hers and in a little panflash she saw a pleading, terrified look there. He didn't want to say her name. She felt ashamed for him. Of him. Maybe she'd never seen real weakness in him before. It turned her stomach a little. She suddenly wanted to hurt him. But before she could figure out how, the look in his eyes passed. Cool came into him and the light squeezed in around his heavy shoulders like a flex in the air and he said the girl's name without a trace of emotion. Monica wanted to grab those ball-shaped humps of shoulder and straddle him and fuck his brains out right there. She was pregnant and for those few months there were moments like that, throbs of inchoate, consumptive, fundamental LUST. She drained her glass of red wine at a swallow and squeezed her thighs together under the table and it, too, passed. His eyes flipped between hers and her tits in that sweater for the rest of the meal.

So she knew Jacob wouldn't have given the little ho who was now in her parking lot a second glance. Her little girl's voice was curling up into the air, unraveling, gathering volume, velocity, and ferocity as it rolled up into the thinning sky.

"Fuck you, asshole," she was yelling.

The boy threw his hands in the air and turned away.

"Oh, no," the girl called out, "You are NOT walking away from me after what you just said to me, you arrogant dick. Do you hear me, John? Do you, huh? You pussy. You...you faggot."

The boy kept going, turning up the pavement and walking down the middle of the lot, toward the sun, although he probably didn't know it. He laced his fingers together and hung his arms on top of his skull, shaking his head as he walked. The girl came around the corner of the car and ran after him as fast as she could in those heels, yelling. The boy started up a stairway between two of the carports, a stairway that led to a patch of packed dirt and Bermuda grass where the people in the building all took their dogs to shit.

The girl caught up with him as he took the stairs two at a time and gave him a two-handed shove on the ass. She lost her balance, too, and together they stumbled down onto the concrete steps.

Monica felt a smile tighten her cheeks. She let her eyes close, like a slow blink. She pulled the warm summer air in through her nostrils and felt her nares flare like she was wrapping up a yoga class and her mind found the memory she wanted to match the moisture in the strange, early air.

I am behind you. I am drunk and you, my love, you are a man, drunker than me, your arms are bare in that-shirt with the little sleeves that I love so much. I have been leaning my head against the passenger-side window in your car, watching your arms on the steering wheel. You actually have a farmer's tan. It's a big bench seat, vinyl. You were sliding that huge, old car over the streets and I am not sure how they got so wet. It hasn't rained. I can't remember where we've been, but now we are home, at your place—the old, brick place you had in midtown with the balcony and the tall white colonnades and the galley kitchen. I am behind you on the uneven wooden stairs. The railings have great, thick coats of cream-colored paint on top of paint on top of paint. The woodwork and the walls are the same cream color and everything is crooked and out of whack. Your butt looks good. So I lean forward and give it a little bite. Maybe too much. I am drunk. You slap my face. A knee-jerk reaction and even I know it, but when you turn your eyes are filled with apology and for a second I'm afraid you might cry and fuck up the whole moment, because when your hand popped my cheek a little synapse sent it straight down to the center of me and I felt like a strobe light lit up the deepest part of my pussy, my womb, my gut. So I take a step up the stairs and before you can say anything I let my hand float up and snap across your face with almost everything I have and you grab my cheek with your thumb on my jaw and your rough palm pressing against the side of my neck and kiss me in a way that makes me feel like you are just barely able to keep from consuming me, from stealing the air from inside my lungs. I don't even know if we closed the apartment door. It wouldn't have mattered because we were loud and there are no walls to damp the noise that I made that night. It must have been like a light that burst forth from my throat. I felt like I had vomited burning sun and like the stuff in my organs had been squeezed out like a toothpaste tube. You acted weird for days after that. I was sore in the anonymous muscles of my hips and back and belly.

Monica did not open her eyes. She did not stop breathing. The kids down in the parking lot were making noise but something was muddling it. She thought, maybe the sun is slipping over the treetops. There were ashes and lindens and a sweetgum whose smell she had never noticed until that second. When Jacob lost his lease on the little apartment in Midtown, they'd rented a big shirtwaist house in a shit neighborhood because he loved it there, around the Mexicans, their round little women, their food smells in the summer, their awful music and their huge clownish cars. She loved it, too.

There was a sweetgum in the tree lawn and a stained glass window in the stairway and there was a grain pattern in the tiger oak balustrade and she could call to mind the details of that stairway, down to the number of stairs and which ones creaked and the third one above the landing had a cigarette burn in the runner that looked like an eye. But she couldn't, could not recall the whole denouement part of their relationship with anything but the vaguest chronology. In this light she was in now, light that grows by the blink but never changes when you look into it, she knew that was the part he must remember most vividly—her coldness, all the phone calls, his yowling, his abject begging, how she'd felt herself harden as he prostrated because it was the only way she could maintain his dignity for him and preserve her memory of him as a man and not a simpering pussy. She knew he dwelt on these things for a long time after and probably still does now and again. But Monica remembered only a few things and those very rarely and a lot of them were things she remembered with her fingertips and her palms and her skin and the part of the human being that is not a mind or a heart or a soul or a vagina but a kind of marker in the spaces of time and whose only manifestation is the pushes and the pulses in the light behind us, around us, in us.

*   *   *

Monica opened her eyes and the kids were sitting, the girl in the boy's arms, sobbing. He reached up and wiped a tear from his own eye. The sun was in the linden. The shape of the world to come was obvious. The boy whispered something to the girl and pointed at Monica. She followed his finger and rose to her feet, tossing her little fists down at her sides like a toddler.

"Mind your own business, bitch," she yelled. The boy stood and shushed her and began to usher her back toward the apartment building. Monica noticed an old sedan parked under the awning and she squinted into the darker shadows there, where the night was cowering still. Maybe there was a man's head on the driver's side. Maybe. It was hard to tell. She had leaned half out the window to crane her neck and she felt a little breeze tease the collar of her t-shirt. She looked down and the V-neck of it had opened and swung down revealing her right nipple. She tugged the collar back into place up and stood up back inside her window. She padded down the hallway to the bathroom to brush her teeth.

Afterwards she peed, ran a cup of water from the tap, pinched her pill from the little pill wheel and swallowed it. She could taste the river in the water. When she lay down, the end of night gave in—collapsing around her—and it was suddenly the real, open morning. She pulled the light cotton sheet over her, bright white and unscented of men or history. Clean. Slightly chloric. With a breath, rest came into her body and right before the blue corners of her room faded away to sleep and truer dreams she felt his shoulders in her shoulders and the pull of their weight tugging at her neck muscles. And then she felt it dissipate like sweat from her forearms after a jog, when the breeze is warm but dry.

Fire the Men Who Made the Moon

LIKE YOU—and your heroes—I, too, once believed in such things. As heroes. We were all of us wrong. I was your age. And when I was, a string of twenty-something strangers brought me wine and soft-pack cigarettes in brown paper bags, crinkled about the neck. The off-white wedding dress of a born-again bride. Gripped in fists young, eager and angry. These boyish men—each of them, it now seems, dusted with fine new mustaches—they returned to the parking lots of my adolescence with sweated fifths of vile and acrid distillate. These, I thought, were heroes. My heroes would never lend me a light. Under ill and amber neon, atop blacktop, squatting on curbs and nervously surveying approaching traffic for the grille of a Ford hunched beneath the dark coffin of police lights, I awaited the resurrection of stillborn sirens. Not once did they come. For this small dispensation I anointed these young men saints, and forgave them the change they kept for themselves, often a larger purse than was spent within on vices delivered without to my waiting, pocketed hands.

I have outgrown these newly-minted men, now. I wear them in the paunch and punches of my people. I pay them to rake the leaves from my yard. I became a man. And when I did, I forgot the wispy, disheveled idling in the parking lots. I forgot their postures and their clutching, bald knuckles. I have arrived at my days on the porch of a small house, and buy my drink at tavern on weeknights. So I was almost unable to comprehend one afternoon some years ago when one of two young boys, milling about the parking lot of a gas station, offered up a crumpled bill as I passed, and asked would I buy him a pack of cigarettes. I said no, and cast about for a cigarette saint perched in the knave.

"I'll light you a candle, son," I said to the pavement, and may have slowly shook my head.

"Go fuck yourself," is what I think he said.

That boy is probably old enough to buy his own cigarettes now. Too young, though, to offer one to the half-Mexican from Kansas City he buys weed from. As they rise from the table. To stand and stretch in the shade outside the last drive-in hamburger stand in Iola, watching the economy cars of community college kids cut on their headlamps as they drive east. Sweating down the hollow of his back. And when the offer is politely declined with a wave, that boy is still probably too young yet to say something like, yeah, I don't really like the fucking things, either.

He would be just old enough to need to shave by now. Probably trying to decide whether or not to cut his hair before this job interview. But he is not yet on his third vodka tonic of the afternoon, drunk from his knees up. His bony frame still awaits the days' discomfort of a hard hat, or a barstool. Son, there can be no respite on or within thin women. This he will discover. Someday. So will the other kid. The one who was riding a bike in loping circles around the parking lot, waiting for the littler one to score the cigarettes. Had any of us known—that day—that I could, over a cigarette and a beer, trace the lines of their lives out for them with a stick in the sand at the curb, maybe we'd all be better off.

Look here, kid, I could've said to the one with the bike. You'll take work in construction. Just bullshit at first, back work. Of course, they got another name for it. The Mexicans will snicker when they hear that. Now, if you work as hard as the laziest one of them Mexicans—which'll be hard to do—you'll start getting cut work under the carpenters. Then you'll get a union-wage work, and you don't have to say construction worker when someone asks what you do. Say, I'm a carpenter. You can tell girls that.

But none of us knew. And I mistrusted his slick, social little friend…go fuck your own self, kid. And maybe I'm wrong, anyway. Maybe he's at a state school, with no worries about the length of his hair, or the chip in his front tooth that he broke when he fell off the bike that day. How he never fixed it because he could tuck the filter into the gap. How this trick eventually leads him to work as a carpenter, laying out forms on a bridge crew, after he drops out of college. How it leads him there ought to be clear. And how.

Anyway, he got his cigarette after all. The cigarette was offered after the bigger kid laid his bike over in a wash of sand by the sewer grate. To his credit, he accepted the cigarette as though he'd reached one out of a soft pack before, as passive as was its offering up. And already he didn't cry, that big son of a bitch. He just lay there on the asphalt for a little while, as fresh blood started from his palm, his knee, his chin.

Of course, kid…we were proud ones, too. Once. For you then, I remember these few times: smoking, supine, big sweep of smile, and an ashtray propped on my first beer gut, looking at the screws in the light fixture, feeling like I could make it. Like a different life. Like the bruises would heal.

When he fell, an older woman ran as best she could in those shoes to see if the kid was all right. The littler kid came running too, but nearly forgot why when he bumped into the older woman, and her breast flattened against his shoulder.

She asked the big one was he all right, leaning over him. The littler kid tried to position himself to see down her shirt, and did. He was—as the kids say—a winner. Always for him there'd be the sneak of cleavage, the easy glide of flesh and fat across ribs and sternum. The fallen kid spit out the piece of his tooth, and said he'd be all right. The woman helped him up, and the little kid was almost relieved when he could no longer see the slope of beige lace and mismatched tan line telling tit.

The big kid was all right. The woman pampered him a little anyway. She smoothed his hair back from his forehead. She tilted her head to the right.

The door clanged open and the woman's husband called out to her, walking stiff-kneed across the little parking lot.

"Maggie?"

I watched him squint, and lift a hand to block the sun.

Margaret explained across the parking lot, lowering her voice as her husband neared. When he was close enough, she was talking just above the traffic.

"Shit," he said looking the big kid up and down. The little kid picked up the bike and the big kid dusted himself off. The husband reached into the inside of his sport coat and pulled out a pack of cigarettes. He shook out two and held the pack out to the big kid who had fallen, without thinking. Later he would regret it, and the way his wife looked at him in the car afterwards. The big kid took it without a thank you and smiled his new smile. The chip in his tooth took years off his face, but it was too late to not offer a light.

"Just…don't smoke it here. You know—the gas," shrugged Maggie's husband.

She called some one of them honey, and they all left out slowly by twos, muttering ones to the others. When Maggie and her husband got home, she pushed his hand away from her breast, but didn't scoot over to the other side of the couch. It was Sunday, and in the afternoon on Sundays, after church, they habituated on the couch without taking off all their clothes.

When he is older, the big kid will be denied access to an untold cache of second date capitulations because of the linger of cigarette smoke in his mouth and clothes and hair. Another time, though, maybe he'll take a drag and blow a kiss of smoke at a girl sitting Indian-style on the floor. She will giggle and lilt. If he brushes off her gushing, if he feigns aloofness like a dyke against all his urge to spin interested, if the needle touches down like the passage of a season…then she will, after some fawning, allow herself. On the couch that afternoon, Maggie's husband would likewise find himself remanded to quotidian circumstance. Accused by the chip-toothed grin. Remitted, after some huffing, by the palled grace of perfunction.

And me—did I pause in the door? A perfect profile against the tape stuck to the doorjamb, recording my height and cutting a figure for the security cameras? Did I read those lips from within the glass, asking for ten on Pump 4 without looking at the obese and greasy boogan behind the counter, sliding a twenty, palmdown, across the pen-scarred countertop and rolling my palm over to await my change? Or was I walking among you, disguised as litter skittered by the light wind? Might I not also have seen as you saw? That I am the humors of your eyes, boys? Must your visions pass through me first like light through a mixed drink, muddled by the intoxicants I hold, ready for release into the kinetic, bumbling world in which we will reel and collide against one and other for almost ever?

I tell you. I am not the flattened tit. I am not the basement apartments of your low lonesome. Nor the shoes, which pinch your pinky toes, as you walk up the aisles with your serial brides. No, sons and husbands, I am only the old man silently mouthing the words to a song in the dusk where the bar curves toward the narrow hall to the pisser. Rather, the downy-lipped and pimpled youth, leaned back against the hood of a rusted, tinny import, parked for all time on the gravel lot where you say you fingered Margaret Mullins after the children were called home from their teeter-tottering at sunset. Maybe you should have waited till I left, too. To order a round for the bar, to peel aside the lacey panties she washes herself and never throws into the laundry with her cartooned PJs and her father's yellowing t-shirts. But how could you possibly know that I existed—then as now—as the inconsequence of your world. Mute and mad. With only my presence to offer. As I have lived and will live all your lives, tucked into the overhead luggage rack and spitting with rage. I could be your Cassandra, but you've set me under the table as an unmentionable McGuffin.

Boys, I am the we within you all. The conjugation your tongue has lost. Yet still I am with you—you nameless, you emasculated, you jealous, proud, and cut down. You starting blood from our wounds, and looking down her shirt like a boy like a man. Enraptured, erupting, smoking coolly and walking away from Maggie, who looked serene and maternal and a lot like something I've called by many names...

Mary (the smell of fried flowers).

Eleanor (moonlight the color of your thighs in the moonlight).

Laura (who laughed slim cigarettes).

Delia (*dice el viento: he viajado toda mi vida pa' pasarte*).

Monica (imaginary Monica).

Helen (I never should have spoken your name aloud).

Maggie...all these frightening and empty lulls. You and your beige lace, your brassiere of subdued and churchy discomfort. These boys and I and your fifty-dollar-haircut hubby will chase the spaces between us, Maggie. We will come again to this place, and again and again. Each of us smoking cigarettes and passing a jug of dago red, lost somewhere amongst our shared glimpse of your bosom. And we will walk away from that common ground not by twos, but each to his own buckling sidewalk, stretched out before him under the scrubby sweetgums, deserted by everything but cast-off paper bags and fiendish squirrels, scurrying as we approach. Oh, Maggie. Many maggies, you so like the cast of our fantasies caught late at night in the light from the open refrigerator door, eating shredded cheese by the handful, bent into the cool fog in period panties and sockfeet. Oh yes, we will walk away from you, too. To grow old and die, each of us a man and finally alone.

But that day at the gas station, Maggie's husband signaled a right turn out of the parking lot, as the boys made off south, passing the cigarette one to the other and taking turns pushing the bike. By the time I'd filled my tank, they were none of them to be seen. I drove away through vacant streets and even the highway was empty but for me and the occasional semi. These spoke to me in turn signals and brake lights, flashing and bouncing over the washboard highway from where we were to where I am. I left them because if I'm still too long, I can watch everything I was ever afraid of settle down on my life like dust in the light through venetian blinds.

I know them because I left them. As you must now know me. But even in this new place, another brand-new Indianapolis, the boys practice the long wait for death in the parking lots of gas stations. Even here the men grow tired of always having to drive and never getting to have the couch to themselves. Here the old fears, crippling and biblical, have followed me. I'm scared of cigarettes, of bicycles and chipped-tooth boys. I'm scared of turning right out of that parking lot, of a woman I may see, hurrying in high heels. I told you about all this, my love—I think—in a letter. A letter with only two words. Keep it somewhere close. Maybe in your purse, between your Camel Lights and your pills. Please. These same two words can be found somewhere on a billboard, on a cereal box, on your husband's business card. When you see them, that was me…telling you what I knew that you didn't. And don't. And I don't know it either, anymore. But it was the last secret I kept from you. I posted that letter goodbye from one of the anonyms of the middle-west. I think I may have called you Maggie, both in bed and in that letter. For this I cannot apologize. For the rest, accept that final secret as a token of my sincere contrition. Also, I truly regret having occasionally taken morsels from your plate with my tobacco-stained forefinger and unwashed thumb in spite of your explicit request that I desist this pernicious breech of etiquette and with very little—if any—regard to my previously reiterated vows to accommodate this simplest of courtesies. I'm sorry.

When I want that secret back, my love, I will not ask for it. Instead I will return home to east Kansas, to eat at all the many restaurants we quarreled in. Ordering the dishes we both ordered and picking from both plates, as is my wont. I will smoke at the table after my meal and I will go fuck myself alone on the couch every Sunday in autumn. I will tell myself the secrets I once told you. I will begin this way. And in this way, when it is done, these things will be mine again. I will. I swear it.

There over east Kansas, two young boys hung a fake moon at the edge of the terrifying expanse of their nighttime. Under this fraud—as one—they dreamed the meta-fantasy of not being me. The stars of that same nighttime now remember to us that freckles camouflage the freckle-faced boy from fate. To exact revenge, the fates will knock the front tooth from each perfectly pale male before his fifteenth birthday and leave him to watch his friends take up with compassionate women who make love on the couch with their socks on and never yell louder than they have to. They left me here. So I left…that's what we do. Here. After that came the rest of my life. And it didn't go so easily ever again. For me either.

So now you know me. And though you now know me, don't forget that I, too, once knew you well. You and everyone else, saying these same things. Saying autumn when you were talking about the fall. Saying, make love. Saying, goodbye. Goodbye, you mean I lay upon you this burden which is yours to make heard. Listen. I heard you tell that guy to go fuck himself. I heard you fucked him. I heard you leave your socks on during. Is that true? I knew it. I knew chipped-toothed boys and men. I bummed your smokes: first at your parties, then at bars, then I stole whole packs from your little bill-box at the gentlemen's club. I knew the march of couch springs. In March, I quit smoking.

Anthropology at a State School

THE TOWNIE DIDN'T NOTICE when the Indian sat down. Didn't notice he was an Indian. Not until the Indian leaned into him and started talking with that behind-the-beat rez accent. Even then he thought maybe the guy was Mexican, or just drunk.

The Indian was real close. Maybe he was just real big. His breath was ketonic and the light coming from the signs was hard to believe. The Indian wasn't sweaty, though in the light he looked flushed and his breathing was a bit winded. He set a young kid's backpack down at the foot of his stool and pulled out a pint, gestured. What was that gesture? It was hard to say. From another white guy it would have been an obvious invitation. From a huge, drunk Indian with that Indian shag haircut falling into his eyes, it was harder to say.

The townie knew that you weren't supposed to say drunk Indian, even if you were talking about an Indian who was drunk. That thought swam through his mind. He reached for the Indian's bottle. The Indian let him hold it until the bartender turned to watch three college girls who came through the door at high lilt. The townie hit it hard then and handed it back beneath the bar to the Indian. When the bartender turned back to them, the townie signaled for two drinks, one for him and one for the Indian. The bartender brought them beers. Lunch-shift college boy—wore a necklace.

The townie didn't hear what the Indian had said so he said, "What?"

"I said," said the Indian, "I bet you're Irish."

"I'm from Kansas," he said.

"Ah," said the Indian. "South wind."

"Sure," he nodded. He had been in bars alone before, with other men who were alone in bars in the afternoon.

"I bet you are Irish, though."

"I'm drunk."

"Ha. Maybe you're an Indian."

"Drunk."

"Indian."

"Sure."

The Indian gave the bottle a little jingly motion beneath the bar. The townie took it again and unscrewed the cap and waited for the bartender to sidle over to the college girls down by the door.

When the townie handed the bottle back, the Indian said, "So Irish, do you know what I know about you?"

The townie shook his head.

"I mean about all of you."

The townie looked around.

"Yeah Irish, all of you Irishes."

"What, Drunk Indian? What do you know about all of us fishes?" he said, but the Indian didn't take any particular notice.

"Your skulls are, on average, 6 nanometers thicker than other humans'. That's why I like you guys. You have good skulls for fighting...or falling. Ha."

The Indian paused and the townie didn't respond. He tapped the Indian's shoulder with the back of his fingers and made a little gimme gesture. The Indian set the pint on a napkin on top of the bar. Then the Indian closed his fist and launched a punch at his own head. A real fucking haymaker, from below the waist. It landed with a boring, natural thud. The townie shot a furtive glance past the Indian up the bar. The bartender and those girls were still preening for each other. No one had noticed.

The Indian laughed, massaging his knuckles.

"Wouldn't it be great, Irish," said the Indian, letting his voice rise to just below a holler, "if it made a noise like in the movies? WHU-PISH, you know?"

The bartender eye-checked them. The blond girl closest let a wisp of alarm dart from the corner of her eye. Let a bouquet of hair fall from behind her ear. Let a puff of wind carry it all away. All of it.

"I was kind of just thinking that," said the townie, and pushed himself up off the stool. "I got to piss, though."

"Wait," said the Indian, "Let me feel your head."

The Indian reached both hands out as if to take the townie's skull. His hands were very big or very close.

"Don't read my mind any more, though," he said, leaning into the Indian's hands.

"Ha," said the Indian. "You all think we have mystical powers. I just want to feel your head. Not in a gay way, either. More like, *what a fucking noggin*, you know?"

The townie shrugged. The Indian cupped the townie's head firmly in two hands, like a chalice. They were like that for a while.

"In a hundred years," the townie mumbled, "they say we'll be extinct."

He didn't know what else to say. He tried to tell the Indian to let go with his thoughts. The Indian just sat there and nodded with his eyes closed. The townie started to wonder if this was more gay than strange after all. He could hear the light sparking across the synapses of the dry bar air. He missed the cigarette smoke that used to shush it in these places.

"Yeah," said the Indian, "I think I heard that somewhere. Global warming."

"No, man. I mean redheads. They say the gene that makes red hair will be extinct in a hundred years."

"Then we will just wait around for you guys to die, Irish, like a word people don't know what it means anymore."

"I'm not Irish," he said.

"Your skull is from there," the Indian said, squeezing harder, almost painfully.

"My skull," he said, "parted my mom in Ransom Memorial Hospital, in Ottawa. Kansas, not Canada. I never lived anywhere farther than Omaha, never even been out of the country, and sure as fuck never been no Irish."

The Indian's eyes popped open then with the spring of sobriety and he let his hands fall to the townie's shoulders.

"Ah," said the Indian, "So you are south wind people, huh? That's already blown by, my friend."

"Sure, man. Blow…fucking, whatever, O wise Indian sage. Now turn loose of my shirt, I got to piss."

He shucked the Indian's hands from his shoulders, ran a hand through his short, auburn hair and turned toward the little hallway to the pisser. The music was huddling in the dark back there, but there were those extra nanometers to walk with him.

When he came back the Indian was gone. The bartender was leaning across the bar in front of the college girls with a towel in his hand.

The townie tipped back his beer. It tasted like schnapps. The music had followed him out from the dim of the hallway and back into the tall narrow room and now it spread itself around. The light from the beer signs pushed through the space where the big Indian and his dark, shaggy hair had drunk the light, the light, the lite beer light.

He sat the empty beer on the bar top and drained the Indian's beer to chase the peppermint taste from his mouth. Then, dragging his hand over the stools, he walked down to the huddle of college girls. He sat next to the blond closest to him. The bartender shot him a look, and he took the opportunity to order a bourbon, water back. Instead he got served a whiskey and water on the rocks.

"Hi," the townie said to the blond.

She smirked.

"He said redheads'd be extinct in a hundred years," he said to her, cocking his head back down the bar, towards where the Indian had been sitting. "What do you think we should do about that?

As a people, I mean," he added. "Not you and I, personally."

And she laughed and told him her name. She introduced her friends. The afternoon stretched in above the shutters in the front windows. Behind him the music gathered up the shadows like a bedsheet and cast them out over everything. From the south, the wind tippled leaves and white scraps of trash up the street.

He was smiling at something she'd said. Her hair was pale and thin and expensively cut. She was young and from some little town that was vanishing, too. The left side of her neck was downy and whiter than her collarbone and the tops of her little titties. She was smiling at something he'd said and he saw a flash of shock in her eyes and her perfect thin-lipped mouth made an O and he tasted—in the back of his throat—the penny taste of getting hit in the head and he saw light and then dark and felt himself falling backwards.

*　*　*

When the townie came back from whatever dreamless black he'd fallen into, he couldn't pull the world into focus. He was on the floor. Someone was over him. It was the blond. Her poached, colorless hair fell in a little tent around his head and the lights from the bar came through it like all kinds of coral lovely. For just a second, he thought maybe he was swimming. Swimming in a see-through sea, like in a postcard. The ocean, he thought, bores the shit out of me. The girl was talking. His head ached deep and in waves. He felt like he would vomit. She was cupping his head in her hands like she might drink from it.

"What the fuck?" he said.

She said, "Jesus, he just came out of nowhere, like a bull. Like some kind of maniac. I thought he was gone, but all of a sudden there he was, that huge Mexican you were talking to, and he ran up to you and his head was down and he was charging just like a bull and he rammed you with his fucking head. Right here."

She gingerly laid two fingers on his temple. She gagged a little, or sobbed. A tear ran down the corner of her nose and gathered at the tip. The light was all bunched up in it and he wanted to lean forward and lick it. She sniffled and the teardrop was sucked into her nostril. She sobbed and it slipped back out and fell onto his upper lip. He ran his tongue across his top lip until he tasted the sea. She was crying gracefully. He came out of nowhere. She just kept saying that. He came out of nowhere. He came out of nowhere.

The Dog Ballerinas

Like all the rest, he came looking for work. He had a pretty nice pickup and he pulled it up to the trailer at the south end of the jobsite. Molly, the equipment operator's dog, began barking. Tim and the Mexicans were walking out across the girders, carrying sheets of plywood propped up on their backs like sails, like lean-tos against the weight of the grinding sun. The foreman hollered at Tim to go see who it was pulled up.

Some of them drove to the jobsite. When they stepped out, they stepped out proud from automobiles in various stages of grief. Mostly the white guys drove trucks. Empty cans could sometimes be heard jangling in the wind that got lost in their open beds. The boss handled these men. Others came walking up from who the fuck knows where. A few rode on bikes, looking silly like grown-ups on bikes always do. These were mostly blacks and usually the boss handled them too, turning them away with a dismissive wave of the back of his hand—a gesture that turned Tim's stomach, but didn't seem to bother the men themselves. The Mexicans usually came in groups, trundling improbably out of minivans or ratted-out grandpa cars. Tim had to go tell them to come back next week on Monday, early in the morning, in case somebody didn't make it back to work after payday.

It shamed him. To be the messenger. The house boy, sent to turn away the field hands. But it was hot. The length of the day opened itself before him. The sun scared even the trees, and a break—any break—from the heft, the sweat and the lurch of weight was worth the price of pride. So he went to tell the Mexican who had just pulled up to try back again on Monday. Before sun-up.

He let the sheet of decking fall onto the hang-jacks that stretched between the girders and shot Raymundo a sideways look. Raymundo flashed him a gold-toothed grin and bent to his work. Jorge laughed *entrediente*. The broad creek ran underneath them. Molly kept barking. The carpenters' nail guns continued their tattoo.

At the end of the girder, Tim unclipped his carabiner from the safety cable strung above the girder and he walked awkwardly in his safety harness down to the trailer. When he got close, Molly quit barking. As he passed, he gave the dog's wide forehead a good rub with his thumb. Molly leaned an ear into his knuckles and groaned. The man sitting on the steps of the trailer got up and dusted the seat of his bibs off. He walked right by the big yellow dog—comfortably, as people of dogs do.

"*Qué onda, hombre*?" said Tim. He took off his hardhat and swabbed his brow with a bandana. He spat dust and air.

"Beg pardon?" the man said.

"Sorry." Tim eyed the man. He looked at the nut brown skin of the man's face and hands. Behind his ears he was whiter. He checked the man's eyes for blue.

"Can I help you?" Tim asked.

"Yeah, I come to see if you guys was hiring."

The man was older, in his fifties maybe. It was hard to tell a lot of times. His hair was gray. His skin was petrified, peeled, wrecked by sun.

Tim wiped the sweat out of his beard and folded the bandana back up. He tucked it into his shirt pocket and undid another button in the front.

"I don't know," he said, "The boss is down under the bridge. Got a yellow hardhat. Check with him."

"Got my own tools," the man offered.

"Yeah?" said Tim. "Better lock them up."

The old man nodded and reached a loaded toolbelt and a homemade totebox out of the bed of his truck. He set them on the saddle-blanket bench seat inside the cab, rolled up his window and locked his door. Tim hooked his thumb down under the bridge where the foreman was and turned back up the embankment. He clipped back onto the lifeline, shouldered a sheet of plywood, and walked back out over the river on the girder. As he walked out, he saw the old man scrambling down the steep incline toward the base of the abutment. When he got out to where they were decking, he dropped the sheet of plywood into place and as the carpenters began shoot it, Raymundo tossed him the big crescent and they set to leveling the jacks.

After work, they sat around while the sun sank behind the modest swale of turf and scrub osage orange. Somebody loaded up the coolers and drove up to the gas station for ice. Somebody else got the money up—bills limp with sweat—and ran to the liquor store for light beer by the case. Most of the white guys on the crew came from somewhere else, and the company put them up during the week in a shit motel a couple blocks down the boulevard. Some of them came from out west, some from Nebraska. A few of them travelled together. The rest got shuffled around here and there to jobs across the state and the neighboring states from week to week as needs be.

Because he spoke Spanish, Tim got to stay local for the most part. When there were no bridges, they put him with a sewer crew, or a street light crew, or a sidewalk-paving crew. In the winter they kept him on in the yard or made work for him in the mechanic's shop. Still, he sat with the rovers after clock-out and drank their wet beer. When the mood fell to him. He usually began to feel light after only two or three. When he felt out-and-out drunkenness slip into his knees and spread warm and friendly all over him, he'd tip the rest of his beer into Molly's mouth, and rise to leave.

The sun was a punishment…until the last. Then its pink lunula of passing resembled nothing so much as the slip of a pale girl's pussy. Then the evening would be upon them—lifting the air from their necks. Then the crust of sweat and dust could be flaked out of beard and chest hair. Then the night would promise respite from the tented heat of August and they'd get drunk—spitting, vulgar, invectively drunk—with pause only for fits of nauseous laughter. Penance the daylight, festive the sunset, carnival the fellowship at day's end. Men making their nighttime noise for one another to hear and contest—carnal, guttermouth, broadbacked or bent, lowly, lonely, classless, shirtless, shiftless, sweaty-lipped, pub-lovely DRUNK—was evening in the summer, after work. The feeling of relief would usher in bald lies and bravado, talk of women, of venial sins, of venereal disease. As the coolers opened and dropped shut again and again, mirth would warm to malice, the songs of sin would meander toward the cardinal, and the conversation would turn to college boys, whores, inspectors, niggers and fucking engineers.

"Well, I'll be on my way," Tim would say.

"The hell you say," they'd shout. "Have another beer, Timmy."

"No, I want to get home and see the old lady."

"Timmy," come the chorus, "you know what? You ain't no fun to drink with. Fucking Dan's more fun to drink with, and he don't even drink."

The equipment operator would chortle and hold out a can of warm pop like a toast.

"Guess not," Tim'd say. "See you tomorrow, boys. Bright and early."

When he got home, Carol and the dog came to the door. The dog had bad hips, and wiggled ridiculously when it walked. Carol had good hips. They were wide beyond the breadth of American beauty, but they were good hips. To lay your hands on them from the front was feeling like you were slow-dancing, barely moving, on the deck of a large ship on calm seas. To lay your hands on her hips from behind was like the steering wheel of an old, cherry sedan on a good road through the bluff hills above the broad river in the afternoon in the fall.

Carol kissed him, and held his arm with one hand. The dog jumped between them and they petted it. Tim picked it up, cradling its hindquarters and the dog didn't nip or even wince.

They scrambled eggs for supper together and ate them with warm flour tortillas and sharp, store-brand cheddar cheese sliced in thick hunks from the block.

"How was work?"

"Same shit as always," he said. "Class?"

She told him about her day, with a little too much detail, like some people talk about their dreams. He listened for a while. Then he tossed his scraps to the dog. They washed the dishes and he turned on the little gray radio. The plastic treble filled the little buff-colored rooms, drowned out the warbled game show noise from the adjacent apartment, and masked their constrained grunts and huffing.

While he showered, she fell asleep on the bed. He turned on the lamp by the divan and opened a bottle of porter. He peeked into the bedroom around midnight. The thin cotton boxers she wore were worn shiny about the buttocks. The moonlight found the slopes of her shape out from the dark. The bedsheets wrapped about her and kicked off and wadded up reminded him of the old man's skin at the jobsite this morning. He felt easy and tender for her, and climbed into bed. The dog followed him and curled around between his legs, warm in the whirr of the ceiling fan and the occasional shush of a passing car outside the open window.

In the morning they all grumbled around. The dog, the man, the woman, the wind through the window. The snooze button, then coffee, eggs, a kiss on the cheek. Carol padded around the floor in her dumpy, morning-time way of moving. Her shorts and t-shirt rode her walk.

"Have a good day at work, babe," she snuggled under his chin.

"Sure," Tim nodded, checking the urge to scoff, and nuzzled her head. "You, too, love."

She nodded and rubbed her face a bit, like a baby. He thumped the dog's sides with his cupped palm, knuckles its ears and headed out. Carol said goodbye three more times—because she was one of those people—then Tim had the old pickup fired up and rolling down the boulevard with the windows down to let in the moist, dark air.

When he pulled onto the site, his headlights found out the old man, sitting on his tailgate. Next to him was a skinny basset hound with its head in his lap. The old man was kneading its ears with one hand, leaning back on the other. Tim lit a cigarette and sat in his truck until the foreman came out of the trailer, stretching against the bruised blue light in the sky, and clomped down the wooden steps into the gravel and dust.

The foreman gave the old man cut work under the carpenters, and he spent the day ripping lumber with a hefty worm drive saw, hunched over the chalk line with a spray of sawdust dusting his upper body. At lunch, he ate on the bed of his truck, while the rest of the white guys huddled by the air conditioner in the foreman's trailer and the Mexicans lay in the shadows beneath a tool trailer. The dog lay in the man's lap, in the same position as Tim had found them when he pulled up. Tim looked at him out the trailer window. He fed the dog bites of his white bread sandwich out of his hand. The dog took them and chewed quietly without lifting his head from the man's leg.

"There's a new guy at work," Tim told Carol at supper.

"Oh yeah? What's he like?"

"I don't know," he shrugged. "He's older. He works with the white guys, not with us."

"Us?" Carol chuckled.

"Shit," Tim spat, "You know what I mean."

"I'm just ribbing you, Mr. Sensitive. Or should I say *Señor Sensitivo*?"

She smiled. He smiled back. She leaned far out over her plate and puckered her lips. He kissed his fingertips and pressed them against her mouth. They stayed like that for a second, then Carol opened her eyes, nibbled the pad of his finger and grimaced.

"Jesus, wash your hands before you eat," she said, wiping her tongue off on her napkin.

He looked down at his hands. They looked clean. His nails were kind of dirty, but he'd washed his hands at some point, he thought.

"Anyway. He's got a good-looking little hound."

"Not as handsome as our Gypsy, though. Isn't that right, Gyp?" she said to the dog. Tim threw the dog a piece of gristle. The dog snapped at the pork fat in the air and missed. Tim looked at the little beagle. It sat between them, looking back and forth. It was growing barrel-shaped. Its head was too small for its body. When she turned to speak to the dog, Tim could see a little fat on Carol, too. Just a little hint of too much flesh beneath her jaw.

"Carol," he barked, tossing a scrap of pork across the table to her, underhanded. She looked up too late and the piece of meat bounced off her cheek. She cocked her head to the side, and looked hurt and confused. The dog scrambled, nails clicking on the vinyl floor, to lap up the meat. He could hear it licking the floor where the pork landed.

"Tim, what was that for?"

"Look, I thought it'd be funny. You know, like with the dog." He chuckled a bit.

"Well...it wasn't." Her eyes puffed and watered.

"Hey, come on. I'm sorry. I thought it'd be cute." He reached across the table and stroked the side of her head. She wiped the wells from her eyelids and her make-up smeared.

"Now, shake," he said, holding out his hand to her.

Gyp raised a paw, and they laughed together while they finished supper.

After work Mondays, Tim usually bought the beer. When he got back from the liquor store, he noticed the old guy was still sitting there. The equipment operator lived in the trailer on the site, and pocketed his rooming allowance. Sometimes the fore-man stayed there, too, when he was too drunk to make it back to the motel. They drank outside the trailer in a little circle of dust and parched switchgrass, sitting on coolers. He sat the beer in the shade of the trailer's makeshift stoop and passed a few cans around the circle. He grabbed one out for the old man and called him over. The old man slid off the tailgate, helped the dog down, and strode over. He was bowlegged and stiff backed. He took the beer and lowered himself to the ground, leaning against the jacks of the trailer.

He didn't say anything, just drank his beer. The dog limped around him in circles. Molly barked at it from inside the trailer.

"Molly!" barked the operator. But Molly didn't quit.

After about ten minutes the foreman said, "Get that fucking dog out of here."

So the old man got up and went with his dog back to his truck. He left the beer.

"The fuck's with that guy?" said the foreman, and no one answered, but Tim finished the old man's beer.

Round civil dusk, two huge women pulled up in a very small blue car. The operator and the foreman knew them from sometime else. Tim stood himself up and waded through the shit they gave him about leaving sober. Tim wasn't sober, but they didn't know it. Tim didn't either. He took a beer for the road from one of the carpenters as he walked past to his pickup.

He felt slurry and slow and a little mean. He was drunk but hadn't realized it yet. He pulled out past the old man and his hound dog, reclining on the tailgate. Something about the fat women and the leery-eyed operator with his can of warm Coke and the perpetual dust in his chest hair was dragging at him. He tasted the tip of his index finger. It tasted like diesel. He put the truck in reverse, backed up next to the old man and rolled his window down.

"Hey, what's the pooch's name?" he called to the old man.

"He never did say," said the old man.

"Ah, fuck it then. *Métetelo, puñetero anciano,*" Tim threw up the back of his hand dismissively.

"I don't know what that means," the old guy said.

"You should call him Floyd," said Tim.

"I don't guess I have to call him at all."

"All right, asshole," Tim said, dropping the truck into gear. The old man cocked his head to the side and watched him pull violently out of the lot.

By the time he got home, Tim knew he was drunk. Legally at least, if not functionally. He could almost taste the vile contempt that had risen in him so suddenly with the old man, and the guilt he felt driving home. Carol had been home from class since midafternoon and had fixed supper. It was Monday nights this semester. Last semester, she had had all day off on Thursdays and the homemaking was even worse—there had been aprons, baking, rearranging of furniture, photos placed in frames. It embarrassed him, their little blue-collar domestic fantasy night. But it was only on Mondays. She liked it, he guessed. Or liked the idea that he did. That was enough. She wasn't mad when she kissed him and smelled beer. That was more than enough.

She just said, "Whew, it's Monday."

Then she laughed like some people vomit.

Tim was quiet, drunk, careful. He wasn't listening, wasn't even there really. He just drifted, slurping one painfully cold beer after another and barely eating. She thought he might have a little heat stroke.

"Tim, are you listening?" she asked.

"No."

It hurt her feelings, and she looked, just for a second, like the old man had as he pulled away. Something about the way the muscles around her mouth pulled her lips and her lower eyelids. He leaned over the table and kissed her forehead, and the look was gone. He was relieved. He got up from the table and left the dishes.

"I feel dizzy," he lied.

"I think it might be the heat," she said. "It was really brutal today. Are you all right?"

"Yeah," he said, "I think I might just lay down a bit."

He took his beer with him to the bedroom, and drank from it in the dusklight gathering there. The dark wadded itself in the corners of the room and flung itself out like a bed sheet and slipped down over him, closing his eyes with the gesture of those caring for the newly dead in movies. He did not dream. Carol looked in on him, sleeping face-up and naked, half a beer sweating the nightstand. She did the dishes. And laid a cool, wet washcloth over his eyes.

When Tim awoke the next morning, he opened his eyes to whiteblindness. He blinked frantically and flailed and let out a yelp. Carol started and woke.

"What?" she cried, "What? What's wrong Tim?"

When he sat up the washcloth fell from his eyes and he realized with even greater panic that it was broad daylight and he was late for work for the first time in his life.

When he pulled into the lot, the hound dog was lying in the shade under the old man's pickup. It looked dead. He knelt down and laid a hand on its ribs. The dog shuddered but didn't stir. Then he climbed the steps to the trailer. The equipment operator was sitting inside in a swivel chair with his feet up on the table. Molly was panting underneath the gurgling window unit. It was frigid. Blueprints were half unrolled under his dusty work boots.

"Uh-huh." He said, smugly.

"Fuck you. Where is he?"

"Up under."

Tim turned and left. He walked the packed clay road down

the embankment, his ankles turning on the clumps the crane tracks had sown.

The bridge was sheeted with decking now and it was shaded underneath. He climbed up to the abutment, calling the foreman's name. He couldn't even hear his own shouts for the din of the work going on above. He poked his head up between the girders, and startled at the sight of a bum sleeping with his back to him, slashed by the light where the sun snuck through the gaps in the decking.

He reached out and poked the man's shoulder blade. The gandy rolled over, wide awake, and began to talk excitedly.

"I can't hear you," Tim yelled, making handsigns, "But you got to get the fuck out of here, man."

He motioned with his thumb. The gandy continued talking, sitting up and hanging his legs over the lip of the cement abutment.

When it became clear the man had no intention of moving, Tim shook his head, flipped the guy off and turned to leave. When he turned, the bum kicked the back of his hardhat, knocking it off. Tim picked the hardhat up, spun around and hurled it sidearm at the man's face. He ducked it and when Tim began to march towards him he slid off the abutment and ran crouched under the girders, ducking around the corner and up away out of sight. By the time Tim made it up the grade, the bum was nowhere to be seen. He went back under the bridge to retrieve his hat from the gandy's lair.

The concrete slab was lined with cardboard from a box of wire ties they'd discarded and there was a child's backpack and little else. Tim grabbed his helmet from the far back corner, and there in the shadow he saw a little lump of fur move almost imperceptibly. At first he thought it might be a wood rat, but the as the dark bled out of his vision, he saw it was a puppy. A tiny pup, too young to be weaned.

"Jesus," Tim muttered.

He picked up the pup, and turned it in his hands. Its skin was scabrous and its fine fur was patchy. He wasn't sure it was a dog after all. He climbed down with it and in the light he could see it was indeed a dog...malformed, maybe, or just some strange mutt—clearly starved and breathing unevenly. He peeled back its delicate eyelid and there was no eye, only a tiny pus-filled pocket of goo. It looked like a burst zit. The puppy barely moved in his palm, even when he peeled up its lip to reveal infected, crimson gums and a too-thick tongue.

In the full light of the sun, out from under the bridge, the creature began to squirm. It was hideous. Its veins shown red through its skin, one of its paws was swollen to twice the size of the others, and it had a second nub of a tail just above and to the side of the first. The puppy made a pinched, barely audible squeal and shirked from the light. His stomach hollowed at the sight of it. Bile rose in his throat when he saw the thin trail of mucous shit squeezing from its tiny red asshole onto his wrist.

He made his way back up to the trailer with the little animal worming in his hand. Soon, the puppy was smeared in viscous discharge and he gripped it tighter to keep it from slipping out of his hand. As he climbed the steps to the door, its whining got louder and stronger and Molly perked her ears from underneath the stoop. She bound out in a single motion and made a snap at the pup. Tim lifted it easily out of her reach into the air and blocked her with his knee. He was there on the first step, poised like a dancer, when the foreman came out of the shitter buckling his belt.

"What the fuck, Timmy? Where the fuck have you been?"

111

Tim started to explain.

"Whoa," said the foreman. "What the fuck is that?"

"Some kind of dog."

"The shit it is."

Tim held it out.

"Jesus. It looks like a inside-out pussy. Throw that thing in the creek. Christ, Timmy, where'd you find that?"

Tim gave the operator's dog a solid knee to the chest as it jumped. It yelped and slunk back.

"Let me see that thing, Timbo."

"Nah, it's pretty fucked up. Probably oughtn't handle it too much."

The foreman reached for it anyway and Tim held it out behind him. Molly craned up gracefully and snapped the pup from his outstretched palm. The handsome yellow lab gave the thing a good shake and a couple chomps. Shit squirted out its ass as the big dog crouched under the trailer and lay down and began working at the pink corpse with the side of its muzzle. The labrador appeared to be smiling.

The boss laughed.

"Shit, Timmy. Did you see that? Remind me never to wave my pecker in front of that goddamn dog. Say, did you just get here or something?"

"Yeah," said Tim. "I overslept."

"Well, I'm a have to dock you them hours then. Lucky you ain't a Mexican, too. I'd a had to have somebody tell you you was shitcanned."

After work, the old man took a spot on a cooler and the hound dog eased into the brittle grass at his feet. Jorge and Raymundo brought back boxes of Mexican beer from the store and Jorge cut wedges of lime with the same pocket knife he used to trim his toenails at lunch. Tim waved off a beer Raymundo wanted to pitch to him and headed home, hot and parched with thirst. As he drove past the old man's truck he noticed the bed was covered in a sheet of cardboard, carefully cut out around the wheel wells and there was a sleeping bag laid out along one side, with a bunched-up pillow at its head and a little dog bed laid next to it.

He changed out of his work clothes outside the door and took a long cool shower, taking big gulps of water from the showerhead. The dog sat on the bathmat, watching. He stepped out only when he heard Carol come in the door, calling his name. He pulled on his boxers without drying off completely and stepped into the kitchen. She was in her plain school clothes, wearing no make-up, with her hair pulled back high and utilitarian. She looked truly lovely and a light breeze was sneaking through the screens, across the apartment, clean and colored with the end of light, laden with the smell of someone frying something somewhere near and the noise of a small, dirty, windburnt city, making its way home to the smell of dogs and dinner, the comfort of sofas and soft, fat asses and the smiles of women in a doorway home.

They made baked potatoes in the microwave and he fried bacon and she grated cheap marble jack cheese. They sprinkled the spuds with chunky grains of salt and fresh ground pepper and spooned dollops of cream and big knocks of real butter into the steaming flesh of them and when they were done he sopped up the bacon grease in the pan with the husks of potato and laid the plates on the floor for the dog to lick and he cupped his palms under the muscle and soft bulk of her big, round ass and carried her in the bedroom as she shrieked and giggled.

He lit a cigarette in bed, propping an ashtray on his gut, and stared up at the screws in the light fixture.

"I think the old man and his dog live down there at the site. I think he sleeps in that truck."

"What old man?" Carol asked him.

"The one with the dog I told you about."

"Oh…They live there?"

"I think so."

"That's sad," she said.

"I guess," he said, but he really didn't think it was. He could think of sadder things. He tried not to.

She reached the cigarette from between his lips and sat up to take a drag. There was a triangle of moon-colored flesh on each of her breasts and a pale line between them across her sternum and up around her neck and around the sides of her torso to her back. Her hair was loose and thick and heavy. She smoked childishly.

"There was this little pup down there, too. Some gandy had it under the bridge."

"Huh?" she said, tilting her head. Her hair slid to that side and fell into her eyes and across her shoulder and over the pale patch of flesh and her light brown nipple.

"Nothing," he said and laid his head in her lap.

Tim was early to work the next morning, but the old man was already sitting up on the tailgate. He cut the engine and stretched as he got out. He grabbed his thermos and held it out to the old man and when the old man waved him off, he saw he was weeping. Tim turned away and leaned against his pickup, resting his elbows on the rail of the bed and trying to stare down at the steam coming off his coffee cup. He caught himself starting to whistle idly, but checked it. Instead he got back in the cab and turned the radio on.

Finally, the foreman and Raymundo came out of the trailer. Tim got out again. The rest of the crew were pulling into the dirt lot.

"All right, pussies," said the foreman, "let's go. Timmy, the other spic got throwed in jail, so it's just you and this one. Ironworkers ought to be here this afternoon, so don't fuck around, get the rebar laid out before lunch."

At lunch Raymundo motioned for Tim to sit with him under the equipment trailer. He held out a tortilla stained around the edges with greasy, black fingerprints and passed Tim a thermos full of a rich-smelling, bright red and orange stew.

"*Qué es?*" asked Tim.

"*Puerco. Se llama tinga poblana,*" Raymundo enunciated.

Tim made a scoop with the thick corn tortilla and spooned a wad into his mouth. It was savory and hot. Raymundo nodded.

"*De mi vieja.*"

"*Sabrosa,*" slurped Tim, trying to blow off the spicey rush, "*pero picante.*"

"*Como ella,*" Raymundo smiled.

Tim ladled up another bite with the rest of the tortilla. The stew looked like the innards of the puppy yesterday, as Molly jawed at it and its thin skin split open. It tasted like the sun in midmorning, though. Raymundo told him about the old man's dog. The two fat girls had returned again last night, he said, and Jorge had taken one into the trailer, but she came out a few minutes later shirtless and shouting at the top of her lungs. She grabbed the other one by the arm and dragged her to the car and they took off. Nobody thought nothing of it until a cop showed up a little later and asked Jorge for ID. Jorge handed them a bent-up business card he'd gotten from a stripper and as the cop shined his flashlight on it, Jorge took off running. He ducked under the abutment, and about the time the cop disappeared beneath the bridge, Jorge popped up on the other side of the road and ran straight down the middle of the street laughing and screaming at the same time. He made it a block and a half before the cop caught up to him. Another patrol car showed up and the officer started asking who they all were and what they'd seen. When he got to the old man, the *anciano* told them to fuck off. It escalated pretty quick and in the end the cops hauled him off, too. A taxi brought him back later when everybody had left or was asleep in the trailer and he started wailing and screaming and woke up the *jefe* and the operator and Raymundo, too—who was scared to drive home drunk with his stolen tags and *la poli* all over the place. The old man was hysterical because his dog was missing, but there was a little puddle of blood on his tailgate and some dark spatters on the wheel well.

"*Qué pasó?*" asked Tim.

"*Le mató,*" answered Raymundo, drawing his thumb across his throat.

"*Quién?*"

"*Ese mendigo que vive abajo del puente,*" Raymundo said, motioning under the bridge where the gandy slept.

"*Por qué?*" Tim asked him.

"*Quién sabe, güey. Supongo que sea un loco, na'mas.*"

Raymundo shrugged and motioned for the thermos. Tim passed it back and stood up and walked over to the trailer. The foreman told him the gandy had also stolen the old guy's tools.

"I told him to lock them up," he said.

"Yeah, me too," said Tim.

"Where is he now?"

"Cut work still. With the carpenters," said the foreman.

"No, the bum…where is the gandy?"

"Oh shit...he took off, I guess. All his shit was gone from under the bridge. That's where we found the dog, you know. It was still alive when we found it, but the old man put it down."

"Put it down? With what?"

"Shovel. The cops took my little .22."

Carol's car was not in the parking lot when Tim got home. She'd said something before she left about a late class, he remembered. The air was still heavy and the apartment was closed up. The dog whimpered and scratched at the back of the door as he unlocked the deadbolt and the knob. When he got the door open, the dog skittered out and peed on the walkway in front of the door. He left the door standing open and the dog padded in after him as he walked around opening the windows.

He fixed a cold sandwich, ate half and lay down to read. The air in the house was close and hot. Little rivulets of sweat tickled down behind his ears and down his brow behind the nose of his reading glasses. He fell asleep sweating and reading the same paragraph over and over as he slipped in and out of consciousness. When he awoke, it was deep night and no cooler. Carol was next to him. She was asleep, cradling her pillow, wearing only boxer shorts. Her hot breath was staining his chest. The dog barked once loudly from the kitchen. He could feel where it'd just been lying at his feet. Carol rolled over away from him without waking. Her shoulders slumped down and her hands were under her head. He went to the kitchen barefoot. The sheet vinyl shone in little traces of stark, wan light from the open windows. The dog was facing the door, away from him. It turned its head back to Tim, then to the door. It didn't bark again. Tim opened the door but the dog wouldn't go out. He leaned out the doorway and scanned the walk up and down the row of apartment doors.

Nothing stirred but the cirri of insects around the little can lights. He shut the door and went back to the bedroom, crawling quietly back into bed. Carol rolled over against him and the dog jumped to the foot of the bed. The warmth of the animal and the warmth of the tit flattened against his shoulder kept him awake. In the heat and the sweat, while he drifted in and out of sleep, the image of the mongrel pup played upon his mind—its dripping, its festering, its slime. Like a sock full of snot and Jello. He wondered where all the fluid in a thing came from and how much could leak before it just dried up...desiccated, like the old man's sun-wrecked skin. And how did something as arid as the old man's face make tears? It seemed like fluid—any fluid—should be conserved, shunted, reabsorbed into the organism. He thought, also, about the murdered hound. He dreamt of its last baying. How could no one hear its howling while the gandy had beaten it, or while it lay dying in the smudged corner he'd found the puppy in? While it yelped and whined, drooling and bleeding on the congealed stain left by the secretions of the little pup? He remembered the operator's dog, shining and blond, slobbering on the carcass of the puppy while the dust battered its skin and turned to pasty gray mud. He dreamt of their Gyp, lapping from a plate of gelatinous coagulum beneath the table as the old man sat across from him, almost brushing shoulders with Carol—who was eating heartily without seeming to notice—while the old man ladled stew into the dry fold of his mouth with weeping pus and stew from his empty, inflamed eye sockets.

When Tim snapped into wakefulness, this last dream-image still hovered somewhere in the dark before him. He was sitting up, panting, with a scream tugging the back of his throat. It was the first lift of dark before daylight and almost pleasant in the room. He felt a sob rise from his chest and a little wellspring of tears filled his eyes. He took a deep breath and let it out the side of his mouth. The tears retreated and whatever had caught in his chest went out into the dark of the room and eased out the open window into the colorless sky and languid yellow nebulae of streetlights.

Next to him, the side of Carol's breast pressed itself into a little bulb of full soft flesh. The dog cocked its head to the side and looked at him. He slid out from the damp sheets, careful not to wake Carol, and kissed the curve of her skull behind her ear where her hair had parted. Her breath was rotten with the morning and her short, concave spine rolled away down her back. Little downy hairs dusted her oak-colored skin, slashed by a slip of pale flesh where her bikini fastened in back.

"When I get home, love..." he said aloud, and paused. The dog curled into the warm spot Tim had vacated and laid its head on his pillow. He waited for the rest of the thought. When it didn't come, he leaned down and kissed the hump of the vertebra that lay inside the strip of untanned skin on Carol's back, rubbed the dog's forehead with his rough thumb, then stepped silently out of the room and began to get dressed to go out and work in the brand-new light of this morning, too.

October of Brief Empire

WHERE THE SUN found him—the neck, the arms, the face below the shadow of his ball cap—Redmond's skin was the color and texture of dry clay. He was from Medina, Ohio. He usually just said Cleveland. He was unashamed of being named John, but since high school most people—even his first wife—called him by his surname. He chewed wintergreen snuff almost ceaselessly and spat into a plastic cup or pop bottle when he wasn't outdoors. He was fifty-three years old that year. They told him he'd be getting his own crew and a foreman's truck next season, so the winter layoffs would be a good time to brush up on some Spanish.

He stopped at a gas station on the way out of the city after work Friday evening. He thumped down the last nibble of reused chaw and tucked it pitifully in. The guy behind the counter's English was completely unintelligible. So Redmond pointed, motioned to his mouth, pretended to spit into an imaginary cup. The guy smiled and reached him down a package of chewing tobacco, the kind ball players used to wad and chew. *Redman* it was called. Redmond smiled. He thumbed his own chest.

"Redman," he said. "Me Redmond."

The guy nodded gravely, like foreigners do.

While he waited for his change, he tore open the pouch and sniffed the sweet, rank smell of the tobacco. He pinched up a wad.

When he turned to leave there was a skinny young man standing close behind him. The kid had shaggy, dry, dark brown hair and wide eyes. Redmond accidentally clipped the kids' shoulder as he tried to maneuver past.

"Sorry," Redmond said.

"Fuck you, white man," the kid said.

"Pardon?" he said. He tongued the little nug in his lower lip.

"You're no Indian."

"Nope," said Redmond, trying to step around.

The kid stepped in front of him again.

"I said fuck you, Mr. Red Man."

"Yeah," said Redmond. "I believe I heard you. Now get the fuck out of my way."

"Is that what you want, white man? You want me out of your way? Out of the way of your manifest destiny?"

The kid was holding an open bag of chips. He held his arms out and cocked his head.

"Son, what in the fuck are you talking about?"

"You're no Indian, I said. Asshole."

"I know that, kid. And neither are you. Now let me be."

"Fuck you I'm no Indian. What the fuck do you know? I'm pure Bodewadmi. My mom lives in Mayetta. Keeper of the Fire, asshole. Neshnabe. You don't even know what that means, do you? With your fucking cartoon Indian cap."

Redmond almost absentmindedly fingered the brim of his Cleveland cap.

"Listen, son, you look like you could be my kid, that's all I know. And I also know if you don't let me pass by, I'll knock the shit out of you. Hell, I even know a couple ladies up Mayetta way. You actually might could be my kid. About the right age, even if you are a little faggish."

The kid grabbed a fistful of his own hair.

"This is my warrior hair old man."

It was just regular white guy hair, Redmond was pretty sure. The kid was redfaced with anger—flushed, maybe even a little ruddy, but white. He was too young for much of a beard, but the few wispy little tufts near his ears and mouth looked almost auburn.

"You're white, kid. Sorry to break it to you. At least you know you ain't black. About half you don't even know that anymore."

"My warrior hair, asshole," hollered the kid and gave it a pretty good tug. His grey t-shirt had the name of a state school on it and faint purple stains down the front. A small wad of spittle was gathering in the corner of his mouth. His eyes brimmed suddenly with tears. They were bloodshot and wildly dilated but the thin ring of iris was clear, cracker blue.

"All right, man, whatever," said Redmond. He felt tired all of a sudden…old. He should have just hit the kid straight off and been over with. Now it was too late. He'd have to ignore the fucking lunatic if he could just get around him and out the door. He tucked a big outfielders' wad in his cheek.

"My fucking warrior hair, you rapist motherfucker," the kid screamed.

Redmond shirked a little at the volume of his voice. He winced, maybe even ducked a little without knowing why. The attendant hit the kid upside his warrior-haired head with an aluminum ball bat then. Shaggy brown hair fanned out into the air and he just folded down to the floor, almost soundlessly. The chips spilled out in a neat little arc. Redmond had forgotten the store clerk was even there. Jesus, he thought, where'd that little fucker come from?

Probably fucking India, he answered himself, and heard a chuckle escape his own throat. He spat a long, brown sluice on the tile by the boy's head. The kid twitched a little. His hair smeared something viscous and red-brown on the floor by his ear, maybe the tobacco spit.

The clerk was still holding the bat. He let it slide out of his grip, tinking a couple of times as it bounced to rest on the floor. Redmond said, "Foul."

THRESHING WALL

THERE WAS A SEVERED turkey foot on his pillow. In the dim light it was the color of the sky opposite the sunset. It was curled around a ball and its grip was forced by rings of rubber bands. He shrieked.

Like a girl, he thought, even as it escaped him. And Niecie, peeking over the edge of his bed, screamed in response and ran from the room down the narrow hall.

He sat up and gingerly lifted the turkey foot and set it on the window sill.

"Mack?" Juliette called from the kitchen, "Is everything all right?"

She came into the room, and the smell of breakfast followed her. Bacon, right? Curling to crisp. The smell of hot sugar, hot flour and fat.

"Yeah," he told her, "everything is."

"I thought I heard Niecie holler."

"Yeah," he said, holding up the turkey foot.

"O Jesus, Mack. Get that thing out of the house. Put it out in the garage with your other trophies or whatever."

"Is there coffee?"

"No. But you're welcome to make some. Or watch the kids and I'll make you some. Or really, you're welcome to do just about anything, as long as you get up and help a little. Anything but scare our children with dead animal parts."

But she was smiling. She was backlit in the doorway, still in her robe, her face in shadows, but she was smiling.

He stood and made a grab for her hips. She spun as if to make off down the hallway, shrieking too, now. She poked her butt out and flapped the bottom of her robe up and he reached out and caught the flat side of her ass with a solid smack. She laughed and turned the corner into the dining room. An ache wound itself outward from Mack's pinky and back up through his wrist, unraveling somewhere in his mid-forearm. He looked at his hand as if it'd bit him and swore. But it looked fine. His left thumb, of course, was still bruised. It had taken on the color of a prairie flower around the first joint and there was a blood blister under his pinky fingernail. The skin on the backs of both hands was chalky and his palms were gnarled with calluses. But his right hand—the one that grieved him so suddenly—looked normal. Then, as he watched, the fingers wrenched themselves into a loose fist, entirely of their own volition.

He sat down quick on the side of the bed, wincing as he rolled the little switch on the bedside lamp. It clicked on. When he shook out his hand the pain flashed up through his arm again, climbing even higher, almost to his elbow. He called out in pain.

"Mack?" Juliette called from somewhere in the back of the house. "Seriously, are you all right?"

He stepped to the doorway and said softly that he was. The noise of Niecie and Jack chasing each other around the coffee table tumbled down the hall. Juliette came back to the doorway from the kitchen. Now Mikey was perched low on her left hip. He smiled at his dad. Backlight: woman, child—a vision. This is yours, Mack Burke, a middle west like they said it'd be.

"Hi, baby boy," he said. "Are you being good for your mama?"

Mikey tucked his head into his mother's shoulder and said, "Ma ma ma ma."

"I'm fine, babe," said Mack to Juliette. "My fucking hand is all."

*   *   *

Doyle got to the cab barn twenty minutes before his shift. He sat on a chair outside, picking at the pus-colored foam where the vinyl upholstery had cracked and pealed. It was cold as fuck. Traffic was picking up on the bridge, rumbling across the river and clacking over the expansion joint. The pigeons were purring and putting. How do they live here, the winter over? Sharing abutments with the gandies, their blankets and boxes. It'd be great if they'd both migrate south. And stay there. The door to Murray's office was closed and the venetian blinds were down on the window that gave to the street. The garage doors were peeled. Heat was rolling out. Salim stepped into the patch of sunlight that was sliding across the sidewalk and flashed a big white-toothed grin. Doyle motioned for a cigarette. Salim reached him a bidi out from his shirt pocket. A condo-yuppie jogged up the middle of the street, yakking into her phone. Her little butt rumpled up—right, left, right, left—under her black tights. Salim turned to watch her make west towards the Market.

"What is up, Doyle, my man. See any of the pussy last night?" Salim asked, still watching the blond. Doyle had trouble understanding him. All of them. They were nice, though. Somalian or Sudanese or some other African strange shit. Who could keep it straight? Some of them didn't get along with each other. He didn't know which ones. He only knew that none of them like American blacks. Doyle didn't like that. He remembered how much his father hated the Kennedys. It made him feel like that, when his dad would say that lace-curtain faggot, even after Bobby got shot. His dad didn't really like blacks, either. In fact, part of what his father didn't like about the Kennedy boys was how much they liked the blacks. Whatever. It was weird. The bidi tasted like shit, of course. "Yeah," he said to Salim, since he didn't really know what he was

126

asking. Something about women. He'd had a couple of fat drunk girls from downtown out to the county and a couple of gigglers. Their men paid the fare. Nothing special. Thursday night shit.

Murray pulled open his blinds and tapped on the window. Doyle didn't even turn his head. Salim raised a brow. He pointed at himself, then at Doyle and then nodded and flashed an okay sign at Murray's window.

"Murray want you, buddy."

Doyle shrugged, pantomimed a quick jerk-off motion. Salim laughed loudly and smoke and vapor chugged out into the cold air. He looked like a factory stack with the sun at his back. He heard the door open and Murray stepped out onto the sidewalk.

"What the fuck, Walsh?" he said to Doyle. He had the incident report from last night in his hand, waving it like it was an English test with an F on it. Doyle pushed himself up. He didn't like being talked down to, physically. Murray held the report up toward his face. Doyle was even taller than Salim, who was standing behind Murray, and broad as both of them together. Salim smirked.

"Who is a Welsh?" Salim asked.

Doyle shrugged.

"There was a family of Welsh in my village. A missionary. You are too from Welsh?" he asked.

"Irish," said Doyle. "American, really. We really don't care about that very much here, Salim. It's mostly just either white or Mexican or whatever."

Salim nodded gravely. Then grimaced.

"Also you have American black," he said. "And some others we don't like too much. I like Welsh, though. They are short, though. It would be nice to have more here."

Murray threw up his free hand in dismay.

"Hey, Walsh. Seriously, what the fuck, man?"

Doyle told that asshole not to call him by his last name. This ain't a high school football team, he told the little prick. He forgot to put out his bidi before he hit him.

This partner shit. Just another bullshit Mayberry move on the part of the city, the department, the chief. Some idea they'd got from some retarded article in some cop—sorry—public safety trade publication. Jesus, these boys never got tired of jerking themselves off for each other. Not that the street cops were any better than the paper-jockeys. They all had their different dicks to measure. So she drove and Mason rode the seat. He was faster, so it made more sense for him to have the jump and she'd tail. It was winter anyway, the boo-boos weren't on the corners in this kind of cold and didn't nobody shoot nobody till summer come.

They caught a A and B in the Market, suspect fled. She rolled hot, but not too fast while Mason turned the dash-mounted computer toward the passenger seat and read the dispatch notes.

"Some taxi driver kicked the shit out of his boss. I got ten dollars says it's a skinny driver and twenty dollars it's a dago boss."

Mara shrugged. She'd take his money.

"Profiler," she smiled.

"Rook," he said, looking out the window as the slums slid by in their sleep. Like an assembly line for rotting houses.

"So, do you practice your cop talk at home? Like with your wife?" she asked him.

"I'll show you what I practice with my wife," he said.

"Please," she scoffed. He tucked a little nug of chew into his lower lip and she thought, maybe.

*   *   *

"You should get that looked at," she said. "I never heard of someone breaking their thumb cracking his knuckles."

He was about to say, no, the other hand, but he stopped and smiled and turned back down the hall to the upstairs bathroom. He ran the knuckle of his index finger lightly up his cheeks to see if he could skip a shave. Then he sat on the side of the bed and, with his left hand and the crooked index and middle fingers of his right, he wrestled on socks and sweatpants, a t-shirt older than his oldest child and finally his house shoes.

When he came into the kitchen, the light from the windows was beginning to overtake the bulbs burning overhead. Juliette already had a stack of smallish pancakes on a plate by the stove. He slipped in behind her and laid his left hand on her hip.

"I think I'm going to stay home today," Mack said. He swept the mess of morning-scented hair from behind her ear and kissed the skin there. Her nape was the color of a high moon. She purred deep in her throat. He let fall the curtain of curls and leaned back against the opposite countertop.

"My hand is fucked up," he said massaging the meat of his palm beneath the pinky.

"I told you to get that looked at."

She looked back over her shoulder, closed her eyes and puckered her lips. He gave her a kiss.

"Other hand," he said.

She ladled another batch of batter into the skillet. Niecie came round the corner at a flat sprint and latched onto his pantsleg.

"Daddy," she screamed.

"Good morning, love," he leaned down and kissed the top of Niecie's head—hair wispy, white.

"On the other hand what?" asked Juliette, turning and wiping her hands on a kitchen towel she'd slung over her shoulder.

"Huh? Oh, nothing," he said. "My other hand, I guess. My right hand. It's fucked up now, too."

"What? What happened?"

"Baby, let go my pants leg," he said to Niecie. He peeled her off his leg and hitched his sweats back up.

"I don't know. I just woke up and it's fucked up," he said, "It won't open, and it hurts like hell."

"Let me see," Juliette said.

"There's nothing to see. It just aches is all."

"Were you cracking your knuckles drunk again last night?" she smirked. "Or did your girlfriend get tired of you pawing at her while she was trying to cook pancakes?"

He held out his hand. She took it in hers and turned it. When she did, the pain flashed so far up his arm that his right knee buckled to the tile. She gasped.

"It's all right," he said, rising.

"I'm sorry, babe," she said. Her hands rose to cup her mouth.

"Don't worry. Just. Just give me a minute."

While Mack called in sick to work, Juliette made him coffee and an egg to go with his bacon and toast. He ate at the coffee table in the TV room. The kids watched cartoons and crawled and stepped and ran and fell and tumbled over one another. When he was done eating he sat back on the couch, but the boys climbed across his lap and over the back of the couch and he couldn't seem to keep his sore hand out of the fray. Niecie sat next to him and leaned her head against his bicep. The warmth of her profile on his arm spread down to his hand and soothed the ache for the first time since he'd woke. He sighed. Juliette went upstairs to shower and get dressed. While she was gone, he struggled to strip the kids out of their PJs and diapers and into their school clothes. When she came down, she asked could he take the kids to school.

"Jesus," he said, "I guess. You can't do it?"

"I'm running a bit late and you're not working," she said, tucking in an earring.

"Fine," he said. "No problem."

He gave her a kiss at the door and waited till the kids quit crying goodbyes to pour a slug of whiskey into his coffee.

Late, he coaxed the kids into their carseats. He did what he could to cinch them in. Pulling out of the driveway, trying to use his left thumb or right hand as little as possible to steer, he felt near agony. Niecie and Mikey were sharing a little box of cereal. Jack yammered about the things they drove past.

"I don't want to go to school," Jack said as they pulled into the daycare parking lot.

"I know, man," said Mack. "But it's a school day."

"But I don't want to. I want to stay home with you."

"Yeah, someday we'll do that. Just me and you. We'll stay home and do some big boy stuff, like go fishing or go bowling or whatever."

"I want to go fishing," he said.

"Me, too," said Niecie.

"Someday, guys."

"No. Right. NOW," Jack let his voice climb to a yell.

"Hey, man. Don't yell at me."

"Don't you yell at ME, man," scolded Jack, shaking his finger in the rearview. Mack wondered where Jack might have picked that up—the finger-wagging. Lately he noticed more and more of the outside world's little invasions. Into his children's speech, their mannerisms, into the nest of their family. The small reminders that, when you weren't watching, someone somewhere—hell, everyone everywhere—was bossing your child around. Pushing them around. Cowing them with shushes and finger-wags and eye-rolls and all the other adultmarket asshole indignations of human authoritarianism. Dear world, he wanted to write, I have borne your bullshit, broke my back for you, swallowed your shit for thirty-one years....Now, fuck off of my kid, motherfucker.

He wanted to find who'd wagged their finger in Jack's face. He wanted to bend that finger back until it snapped.

"I want to stay home," Jack growled.

"Not today, man."

"But my hand is fucked up, too, Dad," he pleaded.

"Fucked up, too, Dad," chirped Niecie. He caught Niecie's eye in the mirror. He hadn't known he was scowling until he felt his brow unravel at her wide, proud smile.

The kicking ends when somebody has to stop to catch their breath. No one drags you off. Somalian, Sudanese, Ethiopian, whatever don't call the cops. Seeing a guy get kicked in the ribs probably don't mean shit to them. Salim told him some stories about dicks being cut off and stuffed in the mouths of decapitated heads. Shit, he picked a guy up once who lived above a halal butcher shop and what they were doing to goats in the back, in the morning no less, while the kids ate muck from bowls with their fingers not five feet away...fuck, a kick in the ribs probably seemed pretty mild to these motherfuckers. So he quit kicking Murray when his thigh started to burn and he had to lean on the wall to catch his breath.

Salim was gone and the garage door was shut. The pigeons were quiet but the traffic above was unaffected. Murray was coughing and crying. Cursing. Doyle tried to help him up but Murray batted his hand away and spit at him. He felt like he'd exhaled something perfectly formed and irreplaceable from deep inside his spine and his core and his bowels. His breath was coming back and the cold air smarted in his lungs. He started up the hill toward the Market and when he looked back Salim and DJ were carrying Murray between them back into the garage. Salim looked up and saw him and raised his hand to wave, then held it there and eventually let it fall back down. DJ called out something, but Doyle couldn't make it out. He stepped around the corner of a new, gray, steel-and-wood condo building and broke into an awkward tall-man lope toward downtown.

When he got to the bridge over the highway gulch he slowed to a walk. Tried to look collected as he crossed over the swell of traffic below, then jogging again across the patchwork of parking lots between the highway and the north edge of downtown. The sun was too low to reach either sidewalk, so he walked on the leeward side. He heard his footsteps, the traffic, some hissing and the shriek of bus brakes. He saw some broken brown bottles and some white vapor rising from wherever the fuck it always rises from. Otherwise nothing. The mid-sized cities of the middle west, like a family of fuck-ups. When will we lay them to rest? The people of this place are hollow and mean-winded, too.

Doyle listened again to the sound of bus brakes and, for the first time in his life, decided to get on one.

Mara let Mason take the report from the supervisor while she tried to get something from the other drivers. She told them to write their own weird-ass names. None of them seemed shocked to see a girl cop, but none of them seemed comfortable either. The Africans always had their paperwork. They didn't hide or not answer the door or flee over fences. Sometimes they pretended not to understand, though. But at least they didn't flirt. Usually they didn't have trouble at all. Now and again, maybe, there'd be a little flare-up during basketball games at the courts up by the old American Sons of Columbus building. Or if blacks—American ones—started shit, the Africans'd usually go pretty crazy, yelling, waving wildly while she tried to take down a report, slipping into whatever fucking language it was that they spoke. Even in English she couldn't make out about half of what they said.

"Sign your name here," she said, handing the clipboard over to a dark-skinned guy in a baby blue sweater with an embroidered baseball logo. He looked to a white guy standing next to him who nodded and gave a little dismissive wave of his fingers.

"Go ahead, it ain't shit," the white guy said. And why argue? They already had what they needed. They had the guy's name, his address. Shit, even his fucking car was still parked right there at the cab barn.

Mack managed to get them into the daycare. Herded, really. He turned them with a grip of the shoulder—tiny, birdish bones, little lumps the size of tennis balls but softer under pressure of palm. He boxed them out, boxed them in, hemmed and handled his children. It made the women at daycare uncomfortable, these methods. They liked the trim new Dads, in the clothes their wives dressed them in. They would not say the word father, ever, for a reason. He hugged his children goodbye if they asked, but when they wept and called out for him to stay, he walked away without really worrying and headed back north for home.

He stopped at the last third-shift bar left in Southtown. On the same strip were two coffee shops and three places with pastries. Moms fogged the storefront windows. They wore tracksuits that must have looked cute on their daughters' tramp friends. Men were inside in decent, cheap slacks matched to peacoats and polos. People ate sweetbreads for breakfast. Mack parked in a lot behind a row of buildings and struggled with the zipper of his coat all the way to the back door of the bar. There wasn't a patch of snow left, just mottled sand and salt. The grass was parched and wind-bitten. The cold found every chink, even without wind to push it. His hands were cracked and chapped. So were the lawns across from the lot. This dun-colored wash was winter here. It chased away the soft elderly, and the handsome young, too. The people who stayed were mostly hard people or else de facto shut-ins until March. They skittered from house to car to coffee shop to car to office to car to house if forced to step out, into the world. A few, though, were unfazed by the season, unaware they'd been left behind, really. It was these that awaited him in the bar, these who turned to him from their drinks and their idle ruckus this early of a morning, when he pulled open the back door of Sookie's and stepped through, blowing into his hands.

When he came around the corner, Doyle clutched the lapels of his parka to his throat. Like a lady, he chuckled. The gandies were trying not to huddle together, but they sat pretty close at the downtown bus stops. At the transit center, a couple young black people were milling about, on their phones, or smoking, retail uniforms visible under their open coats. The office buildings were still closed, but cars were beginning to file into the parking garages. The storefront windows on the street were papered over or barred. The gandies never bothered the black kids for smokes or bus fare. Doyle got on the first southbound bus with a route name he recognized. It was small capacity, old and dingy. There were a couple other white people on it. Some of them looked away quickly when they saw the sheen of sweat on his brow and his quick breath. Some of them never looked up or took they eyes from the window. An older black woman moved her bag for him to sit, but he made his way to a seat by the back door and sat looking across at a mildly fat girl wigger. She looked him up and down then dismissed him with a click of her tongue.

He wadded his uniform tie and his I.D. lanyard into the pocket of his coat. An old free weekly was folded and tucked into the crack of the seat. The cover story was about some big gay parade being denied a temporary liquor permit. The windows were fogged and dirty and the big city part of town was sliding by anonymously outside of them. Even though the route circled around a lot before starting south through the ghetto, he knew exactly were they were.

"I guess this guy just filed a report last night," said Mason, two-finger-fucking the keyboard.

"You owe me twenty," said Mara.

"Yeah, I'll get it at lunch. But there was a skinny involved."

"I wouldn't say involved."

"Just the same, I owe you more like ten. I'm still not sure that guy wasn't a daig."

"Murray?" She said. "Murray? Does that sound Italian to your peckerwood ass?

"Okay, maybe a Jew."

Mason looked up from the computer screen and gave her what he must of thought was his winningest smirk.

"Do you want me to drop you off at your audition?" she said.

"Fucking, what?" he laughed.

"Your audition, asshole. The 'big-city, tough guy cop' role. 'Cause you sound like you're trying out for a bit part."

"Fine, girl. Twenty, then. Damn. You must got some Jew in you, too."

"Jesus," she shook her head

"Yeah, I heard he was a Jew, too. Doesn't really look like it, though."

"Yeah, neither did that guy."

"Who, the skinny?"

"The manager, dumbass."

She gave him a flirt punch on the shoulder.

"Give me a dip," she said. He passed her the tin and she thumped it down right. She rolled down the window at a red and poured the rest of her pop bottle onto the street for a spitter.

"Now what about this guy's report."

Mason diddled the touchpad on the laptop. He had immaculate fingernails, like manicured almost.

"Yeah, they've got it in here for oh-three-hundred this morning. Vandalism call. Says some guy tore paneling off his back door. Car door."

"Car door?"

"Yeah...in his cab I guess. Down in Southtown."

"At three?"

"Yeah, that's what they got."

"And he's back to work at seven?"

"I guess."

"Damn."

"Yep. Take a right up here on Lawn, after the church."

"You want to drive, Mason?"

"Nope."

"Then shut the fuck up."

With a noise, she spat into the bottle—a bubbled slag of dross down the slick green side—and turned right after the church.

He fumbled back a barstool with winces, sat. He inched his wallet from his back pocket and laid it on the bar. The morning lady was working. He didn't know her name. She looked like she needed to be ironed. Otherwise, there were only four or five men and a group of three young women in hospital scrubs chittering at a table. The men sat at the bar like birds. Poor, dumb birds. Between unlit neons in the front window, he could see the red awning of the Stumble Inn across the street. They'd be open after lunch. Maybe he'd go back and settle up his tab from the other night. They still had his credit card. Maybe he'd let it ride a day or two. The news was on mute above the bar. A reported huddled into the neck of her coat, spoke into her mic. The wind idled her hair from under her knit cap. She motioned expansively to an empty sidewalk and a row of cabs parked along the curb. He couldn't read the chyron at the bottom. They cut to the anchor desk. The meteorologist was pregnant again. Fucking local news. He had two whiskeys neat and left a ten-dollar bill on the bartop.

"Thanks, Mack," said the barmaid as he pulled open the back door to leave.

Some one of the others muttered something as he left and a short, mean chortle rose from the group.

Neither drink had done much for his hand. In fact, it seemed worse. A diffuse, rumbling ache had crept deep into the hock of flesh on the pinky side. Every time he reached for a doorknob or even turned his palm over the pain lit up his arm. He stopped at a gas station for some aspirin on his way home and could barely get out of the car, even favoring his left hand, whose thumb still wouldn't bend to grip. Climbing back behind the wheel after he paid, his foot slipped out from under him and he tipped straight back over, hard. He threw his hands behind him to catch himself and when he landed he felt his entire right hand snap as it bent back. He actually felt his fingertips graze the hair on the top side of his forearm. Amazing, he thought, like a blink.

He heard a high, animal yelp burst forth from his throat. His eyes swam. He tasted copper in the back of his throat. For a second he lay there beside the open car door, staring at the swept gray sky. He could hear the cars on Watley sliding over the sand and winter grit. He felt the pockmarked pavement beneath the back of his head and a warm rivulet of blood on his tongue. His right hand flopped like a seal's flipper when he lifted it in front of his face, the fingers still curled as though they were loosely gripping a beer can. The pain was like waves slurring onto shore, sometimes slapping against the flat rocks, then receding again altogether.

He heard geese honking from what sounded like right above him, but he could see only the sky, the fingerling tree branches and the parapet wall of the gas station roof. He rolled over onto his side and slowly put weight onto his left hand. It hurt but it held. He planted his forehead in the grit and got his knees under him. When he stood he nearly passed out. Leaning against the car, Mack felt a wash of vomit slip up his throat. His right hand dangled at his side like a dead hen. He swallowed back the bile and slid into the driver's seat.

The fat girl got off the bus in midtown. Her boobs had shook over every pothole. She exited through the rear doors, and stood on the sidewalk, rummaging through her bag as a woman on a scooter inched her way through the front door of the bus. Outside, the morning sunlight had been muffled by clouds and the crisp cold was meaner in this gray. Traffic's never bad in ghettos. Even here, on an arterial. The cars passed fast and too close, though the road was broad and open. At least 45, 50 miles an hour. The woman on the scooter bumped and backed and bumped again through the bus door. People were beginning to make noises. Finally she got around the corner and the bus driver got up to secure her scooter. One of the white kids sighed.

"Fuck this retard shit, man," he muttered, ducked out the back.

"Hey girl," he said to the fat girl, as he stepped onto the sidewalk, "Let me holler at you, boo."

The hinges hissed shut the doors. An older woman in a gray fur hat caught Doyle's gaze and rolled her eyes then shook her head.

"Lord," she said. Doyle wiped the sweat from his brow and the sweat from the window pane. The kid had pouted up his lips and was waggling his head as he talked to the fat girl. His whole torso was cocked to the side. The fat girl had her hand on the rolling rack of fat atop her hip. Doyle looked back at the lady in the fur hat. She had light brown eyes—almost greenish—and a short, gray afro. Her skin was very smooth, but dry.

"I don't know what's wrong with people," he said, even though he knew he should shut up, lay low, don't give no one no reason to remember him. Get somewhere quiet. Figure out this thing with Murray, with the taxi, with the asshole from last night. Figure it out before the cops caught up with him. Figure out what was happening to him, to his city, to the neighborhoods, to white people, to the blacks, the Africans, the suburban girls and their half-grown college-boy boyfriends, to the midtown too cool kind of kids and the gangsters, the wiggers, the fatass firemen playing HORSE in the apparatus bay, the bartenders and the Mexicans in the kitchen, the gandies with their Ziploc bags of vodka and the only old Italians who hadn't yet moved out and the out-oftowners who bought their big family houses and rented them to foreigners and the blue-collar crackers in their Southtown bungalows edging up to the yuppie neighborhoods—the only neighborhoods in the city with well-kept lawns, and even those had been burnt brown by the winter—yuppie yards with leafy streets all lined with big, handsome Tudor homes, houses that were actually a lot like the ones on all those shitty blocks more or less, except all the cars are foreign in the nice neighborhoods and the fares are fewer and they always think you cheated the meter and a couple of them—like that asshole last night—think they're brave.

"Child, don't I know," said the old woman, nodding. "Now all our young people act the damn fool. Need more ass whippings is what they need."

Of course, no one was home. What it was of one. One of those big old places that was cut up and rented out. Like an Avenue girl, she thought and laughed. An iron stairway ran up the side of the place and over the porch to the front dormer, third floor. Inside the door was an entryway. Three exterior mailboxes hung high on the wall where a stained glass window should have been. The millwork was dripping with that colorless apartment paint, same as the walls and the floor. There were two doors with stacked locks and a bicycle leaned against a built-in bench. Mara cop-knocked and waited while Mason stepped off the porch and looked down the sides of the house. There was a side door from the basement that came up under where the stairs would be. A shared driveway on the south side, a walkway between houses on the north. No alleys up here. She sighed and knocked again. Cop talk was eroding her syntax. Her mother taught high school English, a strict prescriptivist.

Mason had a nice little butt on him, clenched up and poked

out as he leaned around the corner. A little ghetto booty. An idiot, sure. But an idiot who worked his legs, not just upper body. An idiot who had a wife, she reminded herself. And a big dick, from what she'd heard. Not that she cared, anymore.

She tongued the little wad of chew out of her lip and spat it into the dirt in front of the porch.

"Nobody home," she called to Mason. He turned and grinned wide, like he knew something. Nobody home there, either. Nobody home in this shithole neighborhood, in this whole shithole town.

His keys were gone. Lightly Mack touched his left hand to each of his pockets. It was useless. He knew it. The keys'd been in his hand when he fell. He crossed his forearms on top of the steering wheel and slumped forward. He nearly wept, then. As he tried to breathe through the smart of tears, he had to fight the urge to ball up his hand and knock the shit out of…something. Instead, he wrenched himself back out of the car. He scanned the ground for his keys.

Then he walked out in concentric circles—like he had lost an animal track in the woods—hoping to catch a glint of metal or even that he might accidentally kick his key ring with his shuffling foot. He circled until he'd policed the entire parking lot. The attendant poked his head out of the door.

"Everything is okay?"

"Yeah, man. I, I fell and I lost my keys."

"There is no ice," said the man. "No ice. We have boy that shovel. We have salt. There is no ice."

"Fuck it," he said and spat a frothy pink wad of saliva and blood.

The attendant nodded gravely and passed his hand, palm down, at waist level before him.

"Okay, then, sir. You have good day. Okay. Thanks."

Finally, Mack took a deep breath and knelt by the side of the car. The keys flickered out from the dim. They had landed dead center under the car. His left wrist was aching steadily now, too. The throb in his right hand continued to press in and wash out and press back in again. Kneeling, Mack dropped his forehead to the ground and lowered himself to his belly. With his left side to the car he reached out for the keys. He shimmied and stretched mightily. The keys remained unreachable. They looked comfortable, content. They were teasing him. They were of the world and the world was conspiring, lately. It was clear. The bar bills, the barmaids, the bosses, the bullshit, the bluster and the bleak season. The boys and their rowdy breaking shit around the house all the time. The hippie daycare whores with their libby judgmentalism. The burnouts laughing at him because the barmaid knew his name. The asshole who busted his left hand with a beer mug at Sookie's Monday night and the psycho cab driver with the wild eyes who tried to rip him off on cab fare last night. Last night and a lot of other nights and just nighttime in general with its different rules and rulers and citizens while the good old world slept in its beds and Juliette in their bed when he came home with her too -tired-to-fuck shtick. Fuck this. This bullshit world and this bullshit town, too, with its half-fag, half-ass bungalow belt. Fuck it. Fuck it all.

He sobbed. Like a bitch, he thought and remembered he promised himself he wouldn't say that anymore. Tried not to think it. 'Cause Niecie. Niecie and her fine hair that held whatever light curled into it. He took a deep breath and let it out slow for Niecie. For all of them, really. And it was all right. Just cold and hard and just right now. Right. Now.

A woman pulled into the pump and quickly dropped her eyes and turned away when he lifted his head, his eyes.

"Ma'am," he said. "Ma'am? Do you think you can you help me?"

She stole a glance at him then hurried back around to the driver's side. He saw her eyes flash in the rearview as she pulled out onto the street. He actually felt something escape him, a deflation. As though she'd rolled right over him in her little rice-rocket and pushed his big, gray heart out his mouth onto the asphalt.

He slithered back out away from the car and pushed himself up again with his forehead. Once he was on his feet, he stepped back and kicked shut the car door as hard as he could. It bounced back at him and smacked his right hand. He must have screamed, but he could only hear what was happening inside his hand. He lifted and squeezed the right one with his aching left. The stab of pain came up his arm like quicksilver into his jaw and his skull and his eyes and he kicked the car door again and again and again and began to wail wordlessly. When he quit, the entire side panel of the car was caved in. The attendant was standing behind the glass door talking into a cellphone.

Mack looked dead at him. The man reached out and turned the lock, then cupped his hand over his mouth and continued talking. Mack turned and limped away up the sidewalk toward his house. He hadn't made it a half a block when he heard the sound of a siren floating up the street canyon from far to the south.

Doyle got off the bus in Southtown, just before the city ceded itself to the slum suburbs, the ranch on a slab sadness south of the old city limits. To the east was more ghetto and to the west was the west forever. He walked away from the lighter sky where the sun rose behind the clouds. The trees were bare and the wind wound itself around and around. He turned up the collar of his coat, pushed his hands into his pockets and drew his shoulders in around himself like a great, gray gargoyle. He left a mouthed motherfucker in the wind and walked with long heavy steps. His hand in his pocket clenched and gripped. Motherfucker, he mouthed into the morning, into the maw of the wind. The bungalows lined up down the north-south streets, with their limestone porches and their squat, square roofs. The blocks got bourgier, even in the winter you could tell. No more chainlink fence front yards. No more litter in the parking. Soon there were evergreen bushes under the porches and the sagging of timbers straightened. Paint was fresh and the colors were calmed. No more purple, no more peeling, no more couches on the lawn, no more broke-dick big American cars on rims and skinny wheels. And here, here was the bar.

Doyle pulled open the door, and the sour air pushed back. It was warm and slightly dimmer inside. Doyle hadn't had a drink in two years, he told people, though he knew the number in months and weeks like the ages of newborn babies. The math we mothers do, Doyle slipped a grin. The place was unchanged, though, since his drinking days. Brown and red carpet, a cheaply-built tiled bar, paneled walls and a black drop-ceiling. The fans were going. There were some nurses at a high table and some drunks at the bar and around. He took a deep breath through his nostrils and held the smell deep in his chest again.

"What?" the barmaid said.

"Coffee."

She poured. He patted his pockets.

"Do you have a cigarette machine?"

She pointed. He paid.

"Ashtrays are a dollar. Pays the fine if the health department shows up."

He took his ashtray and his coffee to the corner. It was darker. One of the nurses flattened a bill against her leg and fed it into the jukebox. Obnoxious music began. The nurses flung their arms up and all went *woo*. Their boobs of different sizes slid from side to side and they laughed with their throats thrown open and the old men ogled and the bag behind the bar sat an empty shot glass upside-down in front of everybody. Doyle waved his away and felt the nicotine creep calm into his blood, washing out the tension that gathered in all the places he came together. Out the front window was a little row of bars and restaurants, all closed. Last night these windows and their doors pushed rowdy neon noise out into the brilliant cold. The bright winter scattered the light and the loud voices for blocks, out amongst the sleeping bungalows, up onto their porches. The noise carried so far in the cold air. But when he'd dragged that fuckhead out of the back seat by his coat collar, the wailing woke no neighbors. And a hand being slowly crushed in a car door made no noise at all as far as he could recall. His coffee had cooled. He left a tip tucked under the ashtray on the tabletop.

Mason was still grinning when she slid into the driver's seat.

"What?" she said.

He just stared and grinned. The little tobacco turd peeked into his lower teeth.

"Oh, shut up, Mason."

She punched his shoulder, again. Jesus, what was she doing? This partner shit was problems. Car 144 barked a call for back-up. 7100 block of Crossland, suspect fleeing eastbound on foot, middle-aged Caucasian, blonde-blue, six-five, white shirt, dark slacks, gray coat. Dispatch copied the traffic and then put it out citywide.

"No fucking way," Mason said.

"Southtown? Seriously, you think that's him?" Mara said. "What the fuck is our guy doing in Southtown?"

"Come on, girl. Do some police work. That vandy call from last night—you know, the one that our guy," he mocked, "beat the shit out of his boss over. That call came in for the 7500 block of Watley. Seventy-fifth and Watley to Seventy-first and Crossland is like, a couple fucking blocks."

"Fuck, right."

She felt herself blush, which was more embarrassing than a simple slip-up.

"Well," he said, gesturing.

"Well, what?"

"Light it up, bitch. Let's get down to Southtown."

"Hot?"

"Fuck yes, hot. What the fuck?"

"Dispatch will shit, that's what the fuck…bitch," she sneered.

"Fuck dispatch."

She held her gaze steady but still felt her face flush full. He cocked his head and cartoon-covered his mouth.

"Oh, that's right. Somebody already did," Mason laughed.

She lit it up and he put them on the call and enroute, non-emergency. When the mic was clear Mason flipped on the hi-lo and they rolled fast as fuck, frightened until it became fun.

When he turned onto Crossland, Mack startled. On his front porch swing, a man was rocking almost imperceptibly back and forth. Mack slowed his gimpy gait and eyed the stranger as he cut through his own front yard. His steps on the grass sounded like Jack eating chips. He still cradled his right hand in his left. His cheeks were tearstained and burnt with cold. His stocking cap was pushed back on his brow.

"Can I help you?" he said to the man, and spat again. His voice broke.

"Maybe," said the man and stood from the glider.

"Pardon?" said Mack.

"I said maybe," he repeated and pulled himself up to his full height. The top of the man's head disappeared behind the lintel that ran the width of the front porch. He had short, ash-blonde hair, going to gray almost without changing. Even in this cold he was hatless, wearing a trim gray coat and leather gloves. His thick brow paralleled the low, broad lintel. His eyebrows were small stripes of pale against his ruddy skin. For a second he looked as if he were part of the house. Then Mack saw, like a photograph pitched before him on a table, something in the man's gaze. A glint that looked like something else. Something he recognized. Not foreign. But certainly not familiar. Something that didn't belong here.

"Listen, man," said Mack, "I don't know what you're selling, but you picked the wrong fucking day. Get off my porch, man, and go on about your way."

"Don't be hostile," said the man evenly.

"Fuck you. Get off my porch."

"No," said the man, raising an eyebrow.

He began to step down the porch. Mack stopped short in the yard, and lowered his right hand to his side, wincing. He stole a look across the street. The block looked as though it had been vacated. The empty porches looked suddenly a bit ramshackle, as though they'd been abandoned long before winter set in. The quiet hum of traffic from over on Watley drugged the air all around. The man came down the steps one at a time. He was a good ten years older than Mack, maybe more. Still, he moved steadily and—unlike most men of his size—with none of the sad, leftover swagger of a former high school athlete. Again, Mack felt a little like he might vomit. He tried to keep the man's eyes.

"The Stumble Inn," the man said.

Mack half shrugged.

"Your hand." He pointed.

Something familiar sparked across the synapse of air between them. The man flared his nostrils.

"I'm Doyle."

Mac didn't answer.

"The cab you destroyed last night."

The man reached into his coat. Mack stepped back. Doyle clucked his tongue.

"Don't," he told Mack, pulling his hand out of his coat and holding one finger up.

Behind him a police siren yelped one loud burst. Mack shirked and turned, crouching a little. The cruiser was nosed into the curb not fifteen feet behind him. Both doors opened and out stepped two officers.

"Sir. We need to talk with you, sir," one said, like sorghum.

Mack thumbed his chest. The cop nodded.

"Yeah," he said, "come over here."

The geese barked out from somewhere above again. Something flittered out of the corner of his eye. Stepping from behind the passenger door, a redheaded cop had his hand to his waist. Mack turned back to the man on his front steps. He could feel his own mouth opening and shutting like a catfish taking on water. No words would come out.

Doyle shrugged and turned away and began to walk off.

"Sir," the cop said, this time in his cop voice.

Mack turned back to the cops and the black one was already within striking distance. The redhead was tracking the stranger as

149

he walked away. He eye-checked Mack, shot his partner a quiet question with his eyes. Just a flicker.

"Hey," he called out to Doyle, "you, too, pal."

Doyle didn't even turn to look. He stepped lightly from the curb into the street and broke into a flat sprint between the Jones's and Sam and Mindy's house. The redhead crouched for a second like a cat and took off after him.

The black cop barked something into a mic on his shoulder and broke into a run behind them. He rounded the corner into the narrow yard between the two houses at a clip, his heavy belt jangling and clicking. Mack made his mouth stop flapping. The passenger door to the cruiser was still open and the radio squawked out intermittently. The wash of traffic noise still rolled over the roofs to the west. His right hand began again to make its presence known. This can't be protocol, he thought.

He climbed the steps to his porch, still startled and slow. He felt as if he'd just woke from a dreamless sleep, in a home he'd never seen before. His gaze slid across the porch. A ribbon of silver tinsel in the bird's nest, wedged between the porch column and the gutter downspout. The slope and warp of the steps. A six in the brass address, cocked to the left like a woman asking are you okay. The air was thinned, as though half its weight had been wiped away. His front door was deep red, even in this light. Had it always been? If he opened the door and stepped through, would the smell of bacon and butter still be there? Where could the noise of his children have slipped off to? Snot crystallized in his nostrils with every inhalation and melted again as he let go his breath. He sat at the top of the steps and stared down the easement where the cops and the cabbie had disappeared and wondered what the fuck to do now.

Right. Now.

Out of the fringe of his stupor, the sirens grew louder. Closer. The noise of the late morning began to slip through the cracks again. The world came back from behind whatever cloud had hid it. This world...cop cars taxied it around, dropped it off at his doorstep. Fuck this world and whoever delivered it. Here. To my home. Where my family sleeps. Mack stood and walked to the patrol car. He sat in the passenger seat and with his left hand took the keys from the ignition. He put them in his mouth like a knife and tugged himself up out of the car. With a grunt, he sent the keys sailing underhanded up over the Jones's low-pitched roof across the street and turned and kicked shut the door with his foot. Kill the messenger. He kicked the door again.

When Mara and Mason rounded the corner from the north and they found him there still, hands clasped in front of his breast—in an attitude of prayer, Mason later wrote on the report—mule-kicking the driver's side door of Car 144. Tendrils of mucus were flinging from his nostrils as he bent to his task, waving like the ears of a hound on scent. Mara pulled the car up short.

"Textbook, bitch," she laughed to Mason and they flung themselves out both sides and drew down behind their doors.

"Freeze."

Mack dropped his raised leg to the ground, and turned.

"Don't move, asshole," Mara called, stepping out from behind her door. Mason keyed his handheld mic with his right hand.

"Dispatch, 262 has suspect in custody, 7100 block of Crossland."

Mack heard the radio squelch some reply. He smiled broadly, snot and tears and coffee-stained teeth. He was somebody else. No, he was himself, but watching all this happen on TV. To somebody else, who was also himself. Sort of. He'd had this sensation before once, after Niecie was born, before the boys, when Juliette came into the kitchen and sat at the table one night after she put Niecie down to sleep. They'd been fighting, distant. Hadn't spoke much for days. Juliette sat at the table across from him and let out a deep sigh and laid her forehead in her hand. When she opened her eyes she looked up without flinching and said, without a trace of self-awareness, We need to talk. He felt now like he felt that night. Like he'd been caught up in something and always knew it'd come to a head, like the entire story was already told and he was just following along. The feeling was like that. Scripted. As seen on TV.

"Your hands up," the woman barked.

Mack raised his hands. She was sure-stepping toward him, reaching down to her belt for the cuffs.

"Turn around."

Mack turned. The street was framed now by a scraggle of branches. In the living months they made a canopy all the way to where the street ended. Niecie in her summer clothes, holding Jack's hand, walking up the middle of this same street at the block party the summer before last. Mack had leaned back against the linden with his arm around Juliette. Her hands cupped to her belly, where Michael was rolling and kicking. The label was sweated off the brown bottle of beer in his right hand, and the neighbors were arguing about when to flip the ribs. Niecie gently tugging along her baby brother like a wagon on their way to the snocone stand in the MacIlvane's front lawn. The sun snuck through the leaves and a breeze too soft to feel teased her curls. My soul.

"Get on your knees," the lady cop said, close now. "Put your hands behind your head."

Niecie, he thought. She had her mother's wide, kind eyes. Even at her age, when she looked at you, you were calmed. Look at me, Niecie.

"On your fucking knees, asshole."

She kicked the back of his right knee and he folded down. He heard the dude cop laugh, mean and dumb. He dropped his chin to his chest, laying his hands gingerly on his head. It was cold and he couldn't see even the gray of the sky. He only knew it by its dishwater light. He wondered how far south those geese might make it before—mid-flap, as they rose from some water or some sickle-barred stubble—the shot would find one out and knock it down. Inedible sack of tendony flesh. Gray as the sky it pinwheeled down from. Plucked from the flock for rising wrong and never to even grace a table. Its mate might circle back. Mack wondered if he himself could find his way back home. Even from this place of penitence, kneeling again at the altar of the world? And if he could, how long? How long?

Niecie.

When the cop smacked the handcuff across his right wrist, he didn't even really feel it. He just saw. The gray world lit up with a terrifying kaleidoscope of electric loveliness. Like fireworks in a foxhole. This has always been here, he thought. The first day of days finally opened itself up before Mack Burke's eyes and the noise he made then brought sense to none of it.

KIND OF FLOWER, KIND OF FLAME

"WHAT I NEED," he said, by way of summation, "is coffee. After lunch."

She agreed, without signaling.

Together they continued walking. The north side of these blocks fronted no homes. Just slim side yards and little driveways sloping down into basements. Alleyways had been left off several miles to the north where the city was an unruly decade older. The sun was distant, eastern and low. Cool dew still lay in the air. What few people they passed were wrapped up in fleece jackets or the kind of workout clothes people who don't work out of doors own. Many of them walked dogs various versions of mutt. Others were lead by more intentionally stylized chattel, as though they could not differentiate between character and companionship.

"I," she said, "would like a long dream of falling, but without the being afraid. That would be wonderful, I think. But what I need—what I really need—are many, many things that I've seen on TV. Maybe vice versa. Who knows?"

She smiled with neither guile nor pride. He was looking ahead, and thought perhaps she had shrugged. But shrugging seemed too mannish a gesture. He wondered, had he ever seen a woman shrug? If this woman—or any other—would allow so foolish a gesture to fall from her frame? He looked down at her to see her face upturned to his. Her shoulders showed no sign of having been set free from their perch. Her breath still cast a wisp of condensation into the air, to waver between sinking and dissipating, as in a dream of floating. As if floating, they moved through the clouds of their breath. Behind them her words were left to shake the air in their wake. Let the next man passing feel the trembling weight of a thing said honestly and lightly. If the next man were able. If his shoulders were broad enough to shrug.

A long night had passed during which they'd lain together, rolled around in the cool, open-windowed room. Here a hammy thigh cast off in the yellow porch light that cut in through the front window. Here a flung-out arm. Here a hand, cupped as if to catch the wan of dreams dripping and dark—like water from a source beyond earshot, beyond memory, without precedent in this sleepy world. Maybe the same dreams visited them both. Maybe they dreamt alone. They no longer recounted their dreams to each other upon waking. They no longer recalled. They had lain together too long to care, or to pretend dreams were important things. But the dark around them was the same dark until sunrise, when it left pulling morning in its wake.

So Tim woke to the hollow light right before sunrise and the audience of dirty laundry cast off in the corners beside the bed, blending with shadows and the quiet of their home. Whenever he woke before her, it always seemed like this silence had just fallen…just before he hauled his frame from its recumbence, sitting up as if bowing, as if retching suddenly the rummy revelations that were robbed by waking. That the hush he found, like new snow, was for the hiding. He rose.

He left her stretched out against whatever world she went to as she slept. Sliding shut the stubborn window, he left the bedroom door open and made off down the hall to make coffee. Then, as the bruised sky healed, calling forth the noises she knew for little beginnings, she stirred from down the hall and they went out, together again. To walk, like most fair mornings, around the blocks of staid, still houses. Slim strips of driveway parted the homes. Cars idled frost from their windshields. The houses bled heat and soft light out into the dim brisk. Soon the day would loose its children chattering to the bustops and the arterial streets surrounding their blocks would begin to pulse with the noise of traffic. But for a while they could simply pass the world by at their own pace. A walk in the morning, a few words passed back and forth. No more than this—a morning walk.

"I never thought I'd put water in a ketchup bottle," Laura sighed from a silence. They walked sometimes side by side and some-times one in front of the other. One would slow and the other not, or one would pause, to match gait.

"I never thought I'd wear those tight kind of underwear that are like shorts, but real tight," Tim said, as if in response.

They chuckled, as it is said when two have laughed together too long.

Soon, they were turning south. Was it beyond the pale of reason to wonder if all the times they had turned that corner hadn't rounded it off a little? If perhaps their passage and the time they dragged behind them like a misbehaved mixed-breed were as the water across the rock, smoothing it like the hair of a child laid down to bed. Beating it ever so softly, and so many times, to tame it.

This corner—he thought—is not where it used to be. This angle we have worn to round. A fold in your sock will walk out to a wrinkle. Now it comforts the callus it made. All my chafes are only the days, sanding smooth.

She was not one to wonder, though. Or to loose her thoughts. Laura saw little need for these false freedoms. Instead, she opened herself to the spaces between words spoken, to the clouds of breath hanging in the air. The punctuations. That the warp and woof were merely means to a seam. And now, to Laura, it seemed that they had sometimes been a young white couple, lost at night in a black neighborhood.

And sometimes they had been black neighborhoods for each other to get lost in. Other times she knew that they were not even strangers. Not even to each other. They were only familiar masks who moved down the same halls, and found the same traces of one another tucked in amongst the laundry piled at the base of the stairs, or the accumulation of statuettes and sundries on the window sills. But because she read by the margins, she knew that most often they were simply drawing breath, exhaling warm and wet into the cool morning air, and allowing each other to pass through the quick mist the other made.

So they made the corner, each to their own thoughts. His mind to the corner and hers to the two of them turning. The sun had just risen into the boughs where they reached above the rooftops. A woman with her hair tied back jogged north up the sidewalk opposite them. She appeared to not see them. She was flush with effort, and passed quickly and at a distance just far enough away so as to make any acknowledgement awkward. She was young and her high hems revealed hocks that were taut and of a color very fashionable among young white people. As such, perhaps she can be forgiven. Had she paused, she may have looked upon them and recognized something. Maybe the sum of all this whisper.

Breeze through the places the elms used to tower above.

More accurate would be to say: she may have glimpsed all the times these two together had passed a lone red brick forgotten here by the sidewalk. Or again: she may have seen in them the thoughts they had shared as they passed this brick, or the words they spoke in passing, or even the tidal volume of their history of sighs. If you believe it, this brick was also from somewhere near. Around here, as they say around here. Believe this, then: this brick was also kneaded from separate elements and fired into a block with which to stack and to build and to again aggregate. And—left here—this brick was also a witness to the people who passed it. But to speak of a man and a woman in this way ignores the better part of metaphor, the part that begs you not to make it. To tell the plain truth. Or pass on by.

Well, then. May your ponytail swing straw-colored and your breasts never fall from their perch, young miss. May you birth yours in brick houses with the light of evening easing in your western windows. May you pass us all without pause even though we go along the other paths.

Likewise the wine, maybe…tempted to let the liver diffuse its power. So with this quiet. This quiet asks that we allow it to speak through us, because it cannot hold itself. This quiet begs us to be both vessel and vassal to its meaning. We owe it a morning walk by the thousands. A merest minute when replayed, when allowed to echo in the hollows of human divinity, will trace out one life which all might dip their toes into. The one life begins not far from this very block. It is both the couple, and the passersby. But only the two might live it, and leave all others to feel awkward from the sidewalks of the world.

Of course, this life will cease. But not in our lifetimes. It is here for us all, in the form of a woman named Laura, whom we shall meet, as all eventually do. Even those who die without ever having looked upon the face of another, even those still asleep at this hour of this irreplicable morning, even those who pass by with little plastic bags of dogshit in one hand and leashes in the other. Even Timothy David Vaughn from Atchison, who woke early most days of his own life to have coffee and be alone. Even those who as boys looked down the shirt of a woman called Maggie or Laura, even those who are women and who are themselves called Laura and Katie and Eileen, too. Yes, these as well.

This is certain.

And if he is the same Tim Vaughn from Atchison, then he once saw a man throw a beer can from the window of one half of a double-wide trailer home being towed down K-7 outside of Bonner Springs. The man who threw the beer can was sitting upright in his breakfast nook, eating handfuls of fruit-colored rings from a cereal box, with the other half of his trailer being pulled by another semi a few hundred yards behind him. Hand to God.

And him just breaking his fast, at about 45 miles an hour, on the front end of a slow-moving, wide-load caravan with the east half of his home cut away like some kind of traveling boogan panorama bound for points south—hell, maybe the fucking ocean for all he knew. And do you know that son of a bitch had the nerve to litter? In plain sight for all to see. Not to mention drinking beer from a can at that hour.

It is the same Tim Vaughn who was called "TV" by friends and few others, and a rounded out woman named Laura, whose life story was peppered with men of all builds and all walks of life. Men and boys whose uncasual glances freed her of one burden, only to lay upon her part or all of their own. Laura, your life is the haunches of packhorses, and your ass is as rounded and strong.

So, she took his Welshman's surname and clutched it to that shelf of bosom and made from such paltry symbolism a symbiosis on par with little he'd ever imagined. They passed a life like two people at a breakfast table, who'd not think of throwing a beer can from the window. Neither would they allow the roar of the highway to deafen them to the other's chuckling. Nor even would they glance back to see how faired the other half of their home, so long as they sat across from each other and their hands touched from time to time while digging in the Froot Loops. Which is pretty much how time found them. Here, walking down Locust to where it stops at 61st, with the sun just beginning to light their faces on the left. The two of them now made this pass together and had for days beyond reckoning, even unto the ends of the earth their steps laid in a line might number.

Like this they continued south, where the trees lined up for roll call: unknown oak, redbud, Bradford pear. You, pear…eunuch. Greenhouse grafting has you now stand as a Frankenstein fill-in for your breed. Like the jackass, able to bear weight but not fruit. You pear…are worth weeping for. But Tim Vaughan has never wept before this woman, though privately his cheeks have weathered the stains of the dying of his mother, the departure of their children, an occasional reaction to popular music, and the rare, graceless, insoluble spasm while alone or driving. But the tragic trees of his time with Laura Vaughan were largely flanked by the sturdier stuff of maple and ash or the sycamore's swift growth and the perfect partial nudity of its broad trunk. Trees that spread for them to pass under. And though the shade was cool of a summer, the trees let the light run in between the branches in the morning, to light the sidewalk before them. The pear, yes. But also the linden, the redbud, the sweetgum. Here, by the house the gay guys bought, a magnolia tree they planted and babied.

"Maybe we could walk up to the grocery store and buy some coffee," she suggested.

"Let's just go to the coffee shop," said Tim, and they may have neither one been listening to the other.

But when they came upon the corner, they turned when they

should have crossed, a mistake whose merits we attribute to Jesus of Nazareth, the son of God, himself a reputed fan of the morning walk. The south side of these blocks, like the north, bore no numbers stenciled on the curb, and was open to the sky above. The trees were planted in side yards and back yards and none between the sidewalk and the street. Here the walk was lined with shrubs and tall wood pickets, and the dogs barked furious and blind from the other side at the sound of soft soles passing.

Behind the wood fence, a hound brayed violently. Its voice was neither angry nor whatever anger's opposite might be in dogs. As with men, nothing is known of the crying of dogs. To know what they call out for is impossible. We can only pitch them scraps, that they might simply shut the fuck up. Long enough to forget the noise of their own dumb want. Long enough to forgive them. To hear the dog barking, Laura must first have silenced the call within her own soul, though. It is said that within her, this thing sang like swift water through a draw in the still unsettled hills to the west. In the wind. And at each step her put-upon heart held rain. Rain that Tim could never see gathering, despite the fact that he had made the clouds and filled them with flood. No hounds howl louder than this silence. This silence that is inside them all. How tired they must be of our braying.

Like all our women, she was indeed weary and worn where she wasn't wrinkled. Like all their men, he was remitted because he was unfit even for guilt. But more than this was the step they'd step in time by accident, like drunks crossing a parade, when they would realize that they had known these things and forgotten them only to know them again and again and again, each time more comfortable.

Now north. Laura and Tim easy in the home stretch. Soon they were bound to see someone to whom they must wave, or stop to talk. Someone in a robe. Someone holding a steaming cup and bending for the morning paper. Someone whose hairy legs shone through the gap between black socks and the hemline of terrycloth.

"Good morning, Terrence." One of them might nod or wave.

"Oh. Hey, Tim. Hi, Laura."

These things happen. From time to time the spell they cast around each other would be broken by the prow of another, an ambassador from the even more quotidian world outside of their idyll. But as it would happen, it would pass. And in the rude wake, Laura and Tim could once more merge, walking on past the tidy squat bungalows, the vain tudors, and the proud, occasional shirtwaist—all pith and pitched roof. This, their block, held forth all manner of wide front porches, the houses like paupers at this hour, asking alms of the early birds as they skittered from the brambles.

The chatter of these birds called up from her memory an afternoon when the boys were young, and they'd stopped the low sedan they were driving somewhere in eastern Washington. The land there reminded her of the unfathomable buckling emptiness where Tim had grown up. The sere town was sown with litter, nearly all of it white and lighter than the strong winds coming across the plain and up the Columbia gorge. They had stopped at a little triangle-shaped park to push the boys in swings. The Mexicans who lived there piled their staccato syllables high into the dry and dusty air, taking great swallows of pop and tossing the empty plastic pop bottles into and among the merry-go-rounds and jungle gyms.

*   *   *

"Here we are," she said.

Tim heard none of this cacophony. No memory of Chinook wind and Mexican men would the bird song have stirred, had he paid it heed. Other sounds held his mind and called him back, though not so far.

"Last night I awoke to a strange sound," he said, turning to her and stopping.

She stopped—only for a second—and took his hand, a way of walking he despised. He shook free of it, but as she wanted, resumed his stride.

"Anyway, you didn't seem to hear it, even though I think you were awake. The noise was like most night noise, only it pulsed. Most of the time, you might hear something at night and it's sudden and gone. Or maybe you wake up and the noise has always been there and is never going away but you just noticed it. That's normal. This was something else, like bugs in the woods when they are all getting louder and then quieter, all at the same time. But it wasn't bugs, and it maybe wasn't really a noise, but more like the pressure in the atmosphere."

"I told you not to eat before bed," she chuckled, and placed a hand on his dragging belly.

Truly, she was a thing beyond the things of this world. To be told not to eat before bed by a woman of Laura's mien was to be laid hands upon. When they say she was kind, they say her kindness was itself a kind of noise in the night. The grift that passes for kindness in this world is a pimp's ruse, and her way of blessing is the only one worthy of the word. When you know Laura, you will not know kindness, but you may be the brick it passes by. You may be corner whose edge it eases. Few

163

of us will know its passing. None of us can bear it. It is, then, a way of giving over. To a benevolence that stains the deed as the coffee the water. To give over. To allow a greater thing to sift though. And it warms the world against its own exothermal seeping. If you, then, are told not to eat barbeque after nine by one of these who might allow you…heed. If you are walked with, then step slowly. Because in the night, as they breathe their deep and stretch out into their dreams of falling, then you who do not step slowly—and your kindred spirits with the celery salt still parching their palates—you will lay in wait and in witness and when you are called to feel this wonder…you will think you have heard it, instead.

CICADA CADENCE, KATIE DIDN'T

WE WERE IN A LITTLE BAR east of downtown, talking about what we always talk about. We like a little elbow room here, in which to talk. To talk about how we wound up where we were. To talk about where we're from. To talk about night—about nights—and childhood and boyhood and the neighborhood girls and nighttime and the noise of it all. So we were talking about cicadas. These are J. Ray's stories about cicadas, even though one of them is probably about locusts. The third is a story about bats. A story that might once have been a lie but now is noise, too.

When he was a kid, J. Ray had this neighbor. Dale. J. Ray asked me a couple of times did I know Dale or do you remember that guy. I almost did. I remembered him like a word you want to say but can't quite. My parents had moved out north of town when I was young. But I spent a fair bit of time around J. Ray's neighborhood. Most of it with a girl who lived the next block up from J. Ray's dad's place. It was the kind of neighborhood where somebody like Dale might make a little stir. The moms mistrusted him. They scuttled amongst each other about his daily meanderings. That's really what I remember. More than Dale himself, I remember the mention of Dale. I never knew what was wrong with him. It was hard to say, really. He was probably twenty-something, then. Not quite old enough to be a townie simpleton. But clearly well past being just a slow kid.

Most of us actual kids were slogging through our own awkwardness. Some of us were molting into grace. Brunette grace. But somehow Dale slipped our pity, with his lank greasiness and his digging fingers. He had become big but could not quit his boyhood. Not the kind of boyhood that tugged at the moms, either—the stupid, beautiful, hairless sex of boys in cars after school. No. The kind of boyhood that is unwashed and revels in whatever it expels. The boyhood that holds forth unnamed liquid discoveries. Beautiful boyhood was now a thing those moms twittered about but did not touch and tried not to see. The leftovers of that winsome kind of boyhood now occupied their couches. They saw the worst of boys in their husbands' slouching. They knew the bore of violence that twitched occasionally in all of them.

It was difficult, even at our age, not to see the wisp of contempt they harbored for us. It was hard not to understand it. When it would pass behind the gossamer and cast its shadow into the husk of their voices. Dale was like the threat that any one or all of us might lumber away our entire lives, right in front of their disapproving postures. That we might never get groomed properly on our own or that we'd just go on pawing our way through the living rooms and blouses of their lives. I suppose we'd proven ourselves capable. But worse still, Dale was like a warning. A warning that we might shirk our duty of need. That we might shuffle along and fail to regard them. Out of orbit. Finger-fucking the offal domestic. I suspect they hated him, that they might love or pity the rest of us.

J. Ray had some kind of feeling for the draggards of our sidewalks. The sidewalks of these neighborhoods that I then thought were full of panty-waists and prisses. The exact kind of neighborhood I live in now. The kind of place that when you're moving out of your beloved, fringe-ghetto, bachelor's real estate and you're spending your springtime Sunday afternoons in a realtor's car which smells sharply of marijuana swept under the scent of air freshener, your fiancée says, Oh, this is cute. Two syllables.

Cute. And it was. Little houses with something of the cottage to them. Pocket parks. The sunshine brighter as it bounces around clean things. New foreign cars in the driveways. The gutters following the eaves and the lawns tidy. The smell of leaving your windows rolled down at stop lights. The few vacant lots fenced into the yards next to them. Children about in twos and fours instead of in packs. Mothers bent to flower beds and still round, though broader round. Everywhere the signs of adult employ and afternoon sobriety. Everywhere the prisses and panty-waists and the J. Rays and a Dale or two and also the bobbing, beautiful daughters. The ones who would drink cherry vodka and swing on the playground equipment when the sun was coming up after a party out at somebody's land when the smell of fall in the country had rode back into town in your backseat and the wind through the windows moved her hair down through your memory for years and years and even then you knew and fuck curfew, you are young and her soft round will never ever. Again.

That kind of neighborhood. Dale was Mill Park's resident maunderer. He walked slow and leaned into it like at any second the world might pitch forward and knock him back on his ass. Which it would've. Plus the fucking moms and their handwringing. When they got together or called each other on the phone, they didn't speak. They just took turns working one another up. Like boys circled around two kids squaring off. Only the moms preferred insinuation to incitation. None of those Mill Park mothers ever hollered BEAT HIS ASS or KILL THAT MOTHER-FUCKER. They hushed about with their *did you hear about what happened in* or *you never know* or *but what about the children.*

Of course, the moms had jobs, too. So no one ever really knew what Dale did most of the day. Like a lot of dim people, he disappeared at dusk. Maybe tucked into flannel sheets, in a single bed, with glow in the dark stars on the ceiling and his big, dirty feet hanging over. Fuck if I know. Like a lot of able-minded people, I was unable to mind the lot of others except where it intersected my own. Maybe Dale waited till dark to slip out of his tumble-trod walk, pull up the hood of his red sweatshirt and begin prowling for beautiful blond innocence to fuck. And then eat. That's how the moms acted, anyway.

Not that the dads were any better about Dale. They pretended there was no Dale. Which is maybe worse. They were embarrassed. Embarrassed by their wives' pantomime panic. Ashamed that they had to stifle a snicker each time Dale lagged through their front yards like a harrow of smiles, spit bubbles and blither, turning the soil of their evening tedium. They were ashamed of their own shuffle and sloth. So they shushed their wives and tossed off little dismissive gestures and generally did not regard, as was their way. Maybe they were embarrassed of it all. Of their cute little neighborhood and their over-the-fence banter and their cottagey homes. Of the unkempt male company their daughters kept. And of whatever feelings that stirred in the hollows between guts and groin. Maybe shame is the province of all men but the disregarded.

Dale, our mothers could not swallow your lustless list and our fathers could not keep a straight face to see you with. I am sorry. Our shame shames us. Dale, you reminded us too much of the deeper human smells. There was no air freshener for the realtors to hang over all of Mill Park. There was only Dale and the wet things he showed us, things we were ashamed to love. The smell of her hair before she showered. The color of night in a small town. The wash of stars that I never saw, for I should have hung my head. Maybe the imbeciles shuffle forth from all childhoods for just this reason. And they hang their large heads not with humility but with the weight of what we shrugged off on the side-walks of 8th Street where it dead-ends at the park.

Imbeciles? I should be ashamed.

Maybe I am.

Maybe J. Ray just told me that the manchild Dale used to tie a cicada to a long piece of string and let it buzz around him like a satellite. Like he was the moon or a porchlight or some other ora-cle of wayfaring to sleep through. J. Ray told me that he used to see Dale pacing, dragging the toe of his right shoe up and down 8th with his hand aloft, holding the string like a balloon and the cicada skimming its loop in joy or torment or God knows what frame of mind and it was the only time he ever saw Dale look up. Now no one can say if he liked what he saw and that's why he was smiling or if he was just smiling like people so often do when the world is not trying to buck them and their tormentors are gone off to work and the sun is tipping through the trees like it was an accident. The only thing I can say for sure is that the periodical cicadas didn't hatch that year, so either J. Ray was lying or Dale was walking around all summer like a simple motherfucker with nothing more than a common locust on a string.

Another way to remember noise is to imagine J. Ray and someone—maybe his brother Elijah—climbing a sweetgum and swatting down clouds of seventeen-year cicadas for J. Ray to swing at with a yard stick. According to J. Ray, this was a variation on a running game of stick ball they'd been playing all summer using hard, green sweetgum balls and the red front door of Hannah Reinhardt's house as the single base. During these ball games, J. Ray chewed wads of sweetgum leaves in his cheeks like tobacco. They played after supper as the sound of the bugs swole. The dusk stretched out its full length and the gum tree smelled cloying and resiny both, like a trolling divorcee. Like marijuana and air freshener.

The whole world was folded up in the noise of cicadas buckling their bellies. These were the Brood 4 hatch. They came when rap music was still wonderful and I was young and J. Ray my friend was part of the pulse of night. All over town was the white noise of our future. The cicadas brought all that sound to the growing yellow nebula of street lights popping on and then they shook it out, out, out. Until the glaciations of prairie lay down into the soft whoam and nestle. The last brood of cicadas had passed before Elijah had been born. Seventeen years this air had aged—casked, corked, and waiting. For baby brothers. For the off-course kids to become harmless derelicts. For the slow to skip strange and go straight to simple. This air had waited—I think—for me too. Me and the cicadas. And the first sign that night was stalking our sanity, that our claustrophobic calm would soon be laid to rest. Evening, which assholes and English call gloaming.

Which we call dusk. Which we disambiguate as civil dusk. Which we name the new night, when the sun has sunk six degrees below the canopy of sweetgums and sugar maples. But we also might say that somewhere in the sound and the leavings of light are the ages of boys. Subtracted from the ages of men. What is left of these we also could call dusk. Though we don't. We call it what the moms of Mill Park say we should. Mature. Growing up. Settling down. We usually don't call it at all, since we are its prey and without our grubby flesh it cannot live on. This dusk hunts us and only lets the manchild pass by.

I remember the cicadas that year, whose collective call J. Ray and me and all the others walked through, into the first part of manhood. The part that's all cock and crying. The rasp of exoskeletons being shed. The first things of the last place you come to. The drone of the cicadas that summer seemed like a call to. We are both grown now, J. Ray and I, sitting at a high-top table within hailing distance of the bartender. J. Ray is telling me about the noise of them and I am thinking of the noise of us, of our raucousness before it was a kind of display of rakishness. When our noise came straight from our balls and we burned with rage and we had been asked to leave and thought it was a fucking invitation. We were sixteen, seventeen, eighteen, nineteen. Noise and nightfall were our birthrights.

The ages of women are not for us to know. The ages of women are lies. Yet here we are, beating these bugs with sticks made for measure. The cicadas look like okra, which your grandma used to make. She did not die of age, even though she would not tell hers. She saw four broods of seventeen-year cicadas and had some spare years on either side. They look like okra, she said. Beat those motherfuckers, J. Ray. Beat them till it's true. Near as we can come to truth, here so far from water. Seventeen years and we'll never see the ocean if I can help it. But the bugs will come back bringing some approximation of the sound of tides. And who can deny the land here mocks the sea?

J. Ray told me he could spit a perfect sluice of sweetgum resin and saliva. The color of empty wine bottles. The smell of balsam seeping. I can smell it. We were there once. We were looking for the other degrees of dusk. We'd have found them too. With enough time and whiskey. But the girls around there were too pretty for much math. All of them. And somebody's folks are out of town in Mill Park tonight. We plan to pull your world out of round by spinning in circles until we are dizzy to drunkenness. We plan to steal your daughters and your daughters have plans for us too.

Maybe we could catch one of these bugs and dip it in the coffee can of full gasoline Dad keeps in the garage and we could light it afire and let it go and sit down here in the full fescue and wait for it.

Wait for it.

Wait for its return.

J. Ray finished his drink and turned to watch baseball highlights on the TV above the bar. I got up to piss and when I came back he'd ordered another round. Like children, we'd gotten a bit too drunk. The rest of that night I only remember in flashes, like my memory is on strobe. Beacons. We'd taken the whiskey and all it left was lighthouses. Fireflies afield. Bugs burning in circles. So.

I wanted to tell you this, Ray. I was working on that bridge crew. Remember that summer? Beneath the Boulevard bridge on the north side, where it comes over the river levee and rides out a while over the slumped slums of Northtown. We were doing cosmetic work, really. Remember the railing and the abutments and the piers were all art deco—big, stacked arches of cement? We were refacing that, where it'd spalled and chipped away. The crew's form carpenters were nubbing out box after box of pencils, sketching forms their fathers would've been able to build by sight. I was with the Mexicans, working the chipping hammer, digging out the rotten concrete. It was a good job to be on. We were working little fifteen-pound hammers out of two-person manlifts, chipping our way up the piers. Beneath us we could see the old downtown strip of Northtown and the industrial ruins. The Morton buildings and the bowstringed roofs pockmarked with weedy vacants and the bum lots. It was like looking down on a world built of corrugated tin, pigeon shit and tarpaper. The tracks ran between us and the river levee, shuttling boxcars and hoppers by. I spent most of the time dreaming I'd see an old hobo hop off of one of the slow cars. Or that the whole bridge would shake loose over our heads and it would rain rotten WPA cement and the iron girders would squeal down on us and the whole damn world would end right there and I'd never have to cross the bridge again into town. I'd never again slip the old Ford through downtown, past the high school and the modest ghetto, into the tidy blocks that Dale'd dragged through. Where I'd seen the sun up in Mill Park and seen the light in her window and the car in the drive and heard the phone ringing through the blue morning empty downstairs. Again.

Jorge had duct-taped four shovel handles together and was sweeping the bats from between the girders under the bridge. The others were swatting at them with *dos por quartos* as they came flying out. The buckets of the manlifts were no more than two feet by four feet wide, poked up in the air like the heads of gangly industrial birds. The bats came down in swarms. Like locusts. I remember them screaming but it may have been me. Raymundo had his own lift because he was working the torch to cut the rebar and the acetylene and oxygen tanks took up the second spot in his bucket. The bats came down screaming and Raymundo swung his lift under the gap of the expansion joint. Jorge was snaking the shovel handles into the crack again. Raymundo unscrewed the tip of the torch with his gloved right hand and sparked it. The next wave of bats came out and Raymundo spun the oxygen valve wide open. A gorgeous gust of flame blew forth from the tip of the welder. The bats flew through the ball of flame like they were coming onto the playing field. They began to pinwheel about, little muffins of flying fire bouncing between the girders, blind by birthright and now deafened by this new singing light of pain they took with them out into the dew of morning. The smell of them mixed with the smell of tortillas from the factory and the auto grease smell of the collected poor whites of Northtown and the brown smell of the river coming around the bend. We laughed ourselves out of an hour's pay as we tried to duck and swat away the little masses of flame that came from all quarters, dragging trailers of brimstone and burnt hair.

Maybe it wasn't locusts Dale was lassoing, after all. J. Ray talked about the noise they made. The loudest insect here isn't the locust. Or the cicada, either. It's the katydid. Even some of the females of that species can saw out their cadence. Katie did. Katie didn't. They say one of them can make a noise as loud as a motorcycle. It may have been a katydid Dale looked up for. I might have looked up, too. It might have been a sound that called me, not a light in the window. It might have been a noise, a voice. Her name may have been Katie. But unlike us, the katydid has an identifiable regional dialect. And bats are blind, which means they are prophets and fair. We are neither. Nor are we like the locust, which swarms by the thousand. When we would roll out, we rode just two to a car, so the wind could have the backseat to herself.

But cicadas, now. They're choral. Like us. Their interval is the coming of age, which is the passing of youth. The sound we know them by...shit, that ain't nothing but a catcall, J. Ray. The males make that noise. The female signals her interest by a flick of the wing, imperceptible to the human eye. The male approaches. If rebuffed, he flies away and calls to her again. The noise of every seventeenth fall where we're from is the noise of all of them together, come courting again. They make the noise we know for evening by buckling the ribbed membranes of their abdomens. The sound itself escapes through the cicada's eardrum. They can't even hear it. Much has been made of that, but truth be told none of us can hear the call that escapes us. Echoing around Mill Park, setting course by the light of our own bodies on fire, which means always returning.

It's all the noise. The sound is just cicadas as you move through the woods at sundown. The slip of silence moves with you. The silence of your passing is displacement. The sound is asleep. The noise is awake. The wake of a man walking. The wait for his waking.

ACKNOWLEDGMENTS

I owe a debt of gratitude to my parents, to my big brother and my sisters, to my wife and our sons, to our ancestors who made Kansans of us, and to this place that has always held me close. Thanks, too, to all my Topeka people—in situ, in diaspora, and in memory. By name, I'd like to thank Lucas Wetzel, Ben Lerner, Andy Day, Thom Didato, Dana Engleman, and Marianne McGrath.

I'm especially grateful to the editors of the journals in which these stories previously appeared:

"These Brick Cities are Almost Over" first appeared in *The Rio Grande Review*. "Mason Jar Make a Maybe" first appeared in *The Portland Review*. "The Shadow Knows the Corner, the Corner Knows the Dust" and "Applied Exhaust Theory" first appeared in *failbetter.com*. "Aisle Idle, We Pine for You in Rosedale" first appeared in *REAL: Regarding Arts & Letters*. "Fire the Men Who Made the Moon" first appeared in *Monkeybicycle*. "Anthropology at a State School" first appeared in *The Southeast Review*. "October of Brief Empire" first appeared in *PANK*. "Cicada Cadence, Katie Didn't" first appeared in *Fifty-Two Stories*.

CRAIG DAVIS is from northeast Kansas. Born and raised in Topeka, he graduated from the University of Kansas in Lawrence. He now lives in Kansas City, Missouri, with his wife and sons. *Ramshackle Wonderlands* is his first book.